MW00329393

A Flair for Chardonnay

A Sadie Kramer Flair Mystery

Deborah Garner

Cranberry Cove Press

A Flair for Chardonnay
by Deborah Garner

Copyright © 2016 Deborah Garner
ALL RIGHTS RESERVED

First Printing – May 2016
ISBN: 978-0-9960449-5-0

This is a work of fiction. Names, characters, places and incidents either are products of the author's imagination or used fictitiously. Any resemblance to actual events or locales or persons, living or dead, is entirely coincidental.

EXCEPT FOR BRIEF TEXT QUOTED AND APPROPRIATELY CITED IN OTHER WORKS, NO PART OF THIS BOOK MAY BE REPRODUCED IN ANY FORM, BY PHOTOCOPYING OR BY ELECTRONIC OR MECHANICAL MEANS, INCLUDING INFORMATION STORAGE OR RETRIEVAL SYSTEMS, WITHOUT PERMISSION IN WRITING FROM THE COPYRIGHT OWNER/AUTHOR.

Printed in the U.S.A.

Also by Deborah Garner

Above the Bridge
The Moonglow Café
Three Silver Doves
Cranberry Bluff
Mistletoe at Moonglow

*For all who love mystery, chocolate and wine –
or any combination of the above.*

CHAPTER ONE

Sadie Kramer signaled left, moved into the fast lane and stepped on the accelerator of her red '65 Mustang convertible. The morning fog had lifted, leaving sunshine in its wake. Humming along with a favorite tune, she turned up the volume on the radio. Nothing better than sunshine, good music and the wind in her hair to accompany her across the Golden Gate Bridge. It was a perfect San Francisco afternoon. Had she not been headed for the wine country, she would have hated leaving her favorite city behind. But her destination had its own appeal. And this time there was more than wine tasting to lure her north on Highway 101. There was mystery, her favorite addiction. That and chocolate, of course, but she usually managed to find a way to combine the two.

In fact, it was her neighbor Matteo's odd behavior recently that had triggered her interest in the Tremiato Winery. Matteo adored life in the city as much as Sadie and she was glad he did. He was the best chocolatier in San Francisco, not only in her opinion, but in the opinion of hundreds of loyal customers who flocked to his shop, Cioccolata, daily for dark chocolate creams or caramel cashew turtles. Her personal favorites were his truffles – raspberry, coconut, caramel, hazelnut – there were no bad flavors as far as she was concerned. And she'd tried them all.

Sadie, whose fashionable boutique, Flair, flanked the renowned chocolate shop, had heard the story many times. Although Matteo was the oldest sibling, he had long ago lost his status as the favorite son. After his father passed away, his mother and siblings expected him to take over the family business. Instead, Matteo had chosen to follow his passion for designing and producing unique chocolate treats. Although he was a star in culinary circles, he was a black sheep in his own family.

When she opened Flair, Sadie, too, had followed a passion. She'd been a flashy dresser all the way back to her teenage years. Even her most fashion-forward friends couldn't compete with the wild outfits she concocted. Her orange and lime green paisley bell-bottoms had been considered an avant-garde fashion statement when she'd paired them with a bright yellow chiffon blouse, matching vinyl boots and a two-inch wide beaded rainbow headband. During her adult years, especially after she married her third husband, Morris, she'd had to leave her wild fashion days behind her. As the wife of a real estate investment banker, she was expected to choose more subdued attire. When Morris passed away, he left her with a hefty portfolio and the freedom to dress as she pleased. She rented an empty commercial space in a prime location and indulged every whim of her imagination when she stocked it.

Flair was unlike any of the many boutiques she'd visited over the decades, from the most basic to the most extravagant. Each time she went shopping, she built a new layer to her imagined idea of the perfect boutique, one that would encourage repeat customers with an appreciation for unique fashion – like her own, of course. She stocked a multitude of colors, fabrics, textures and styles as well as every type of bead and bauble to accompany them. On those days she was at the shop, she loved witnessing the transition of women walking in wearing humdrum clothes and walking out with outfits that shouted, "I'm an individual!" On days, like this one, when she was out on what she called an "Exploratory Excursion," her competent assistant, Amber, knew how to pull fashion statements together for customers. Sales never suffered when she was away, which allowed her the perfect life, a combination of couture and curiosity. Add to that her love of food and chocolate, and she had the winning formula, in her opinion: the four "C's," Couture, Cuisine, Chocolate and Curiosity.

Of course, there was one more important "C" in her life. She tilted her head to the side and whispered in the direction of a tapestry tote bag on the passenger seat. "What do you think, Coco? What's going on with Matteo's family?" The tote bag yipped back a reply that could only come from a Yorkie. "I'm thinking along those same lines, Coco," Sadie continued. "Something unusual is going on."

Sadie signaled right and changed lanes to pass a vehicle going the speed limit. Exasperated, she reached into her glove compartment, pulling out a white mint truffle and popping it into her mouth. Not one to judge character simply by a person's desire to maintain a legal speed, she still didn't appreciate a car of moderate speed in the fast lane. She had places to go and people to see, after all. Adding another speeding ticket to her collection didn't bother her as much as figuring out why Matteo had been so preoccupied with worries about the Tremiato Winery that he'd forgotten to restock the buttercreams the day before. He'd never done that, and it was indeed troubling.

Even more troubling was the tension in Matteo's voice that carried from the back room of his shop as Sadie was deciding between a pineapple truffle and peanut butter cup. He'd clearly been upset by a phone call he received in the middle of her indecision, and he took the phone into a back room and left Sadie alone with her usual afternoon dilemma. His hushed voice had not been that troubling, but the increased volume before the call's abrupt ending, combined with the anger that creased his brow when he reappeared, concerned her. And even though she couldn't hear most of the conversation, she was certain Matteo had uttered the phrases "stop pressuring me" and "you need to back off" and "the winery." She'd returned to Flair with pineapple truffles for herself and both assistants, announcing that she'd be going out of town for a few days.

Now, watching the Golden Gate Bridge disappear in her rearview mirror, she debated the possible reasons for Matteo's strange behavior. The Tremiato Winery was a fixture in the area, going back four generations. As far as she knew, the Tremiatos weren't having financial issues. At least nothing had hit the news, and Matteo had mentioned no problems. The best restaurants carried Tremiato wines, and the wines commanded a decent price in grocery and liquor stores. The Tremiato Chardonnay was especially popular. Sadie often served it with appetizers during open houses or private showings at Flair when she wanted a festive atmosphere.

Ruling out financial hardship, if that turned out to be a dead end, Sadie considered family conflict. Matteo had never hidden the fact that his family disapproved of his career decision. She and Matteo had talked about it many times over excesses of cocoa and sugar. Had one of the other Tremiato family members caused a stir? She knew that Matteo had two brothers and one sister, plus his mother, all involved in the business, a decent handful of relatives who could cause trouble. And that didn't even count spouses. Sadie had never gotten the names straight, but remembered the sister being the second oldest after Matteo.

Lost in thought, Sadie almost missed her exit, but caught the turnoff just in time. She headed east twenty minutes, then north another twenty on Highway 29, until she arrived in St. Vincent Hollow, known affectionately by locals and wine enthusiasts as "St. Vin." The winery's expansive set of ironwork gates stood open. A sign beckoned guests in with the prospect of wine tasting. Thinking a cool sip of Tremiato Chardonnay sounded just right after her drive up from the city, she turned into the driveway and cruised up to the tasting room, admiring the grapevines in the vineyard that flowed out in each direction. The diagonal rows seemed almost hypnotic as she passed by. She refocused her attention on the small parking lot ahead, pulling into an empty space, setting the brake and stepping out of the car.

Since she'd timed her exit from the city to avoid rush hour traffic, she arrived at 2 p.m. It didn't surprise her to see there were few cars. It wasn't a weekend, or a holiday, or one of many special event periods that lured visitors to the wine country. Still, she expected to see a few guests, based on the overall popularity of the area. But the license plates were mostly personalized with some version of the Tremiato name. "TREMCHAR" one read. "VINOTREM" read another. Yet a third read "3MIATO." She had a hunch the main occupants of the tasting room were going to be family. Reaching over the convertible's edge, she picked up her tote bag and delicately pulled it up over her shoulder. Pressing the alarm button on her keychain to lock the car, she headed inside.

CHAPTER TWO

The Tremiato Tasting Room was a decorative blend of Old Italy and Napa Valley Chic. A black and white marble floor stretched from the doorway to the "L" shaped tasting counter, giving the room an art deco feel. Shelves across the room were brimming with wine-themed paraphernalia from crystal glasses and corkscrews to garden tiles and trivets. Sadie crossed the room immediately, lured by the impromptu shopping opportunity.

She discovered books on every aspect of wine: growing it, tasting it, serving it, drinking it and pairing it with food. *No hangover tips?* Sadie wondered as she thumbed through an encyclopedia of wines from Bordeaux. She winced, thinking of a particular Sunday morning when she'd consumed more than her fair share of seltzer water, trying to shake off the after-effects of a wild night on vacation in France. She put the book back and moved on.

Just beyond a wrought iron stand with dangling grapevine-print aprons, Sadie halted in front of a tall, refrigerated selection of cheeses. Although the selections of horseradish cheddar, Camembert, Gruyere and Brie enticed her, she found the decadent assortment of sweets alongside them far more tempting. Next to a few imported tins of miniature mints and fruit bonbons were the finest chocolates known to mankind. Rich, dark, milky, almond-centered, caramel-laden, coconut-covered and liqueur-infused – they were all there. In every respected brand, as well, Sadie noted. Except for Matteo's, which was blatantly missing.

"Welcome to the Tremiato Winery."

Sadie startled at a deep male voice beside her. The heavenly display of chocolate had been too captivating to notice anyone approach. She swiveled quickly, finding herself face to face with a tall, substantially built man, sturdy, but not overweight. He wore his dark hair swept off his face and plastered down with product so it was difficult to tell if the hair was his own or a toupee. His youthful appearance – Sadie estimated him to be in his early thirties – indicated it was probably just a bad style choice. Sculpted facial features gave him a stern look, yet not unfriendly. He was close enough to be straddling the conventions of personal boundaries.

"I am Angelo." Sadie responded to his strong handshake with a cautious smile, stepping back far enough for the refrigerated case to send a chill across her shoulders. She did a quick sidestep to detach herself from the cool surface.

"Sadie Kramer," she offered. "I was just admiring your cheeses and chocolates."

"Both delightful accompaniments to our fine wines," Angelo said proudly. "Please come to our tasting counter. We have a remarkable chardonnay. It would be a perfect match for that Brie you see in the case, perhaps with imported English water crackers and a trace of raspberry preserves."

Sadie threw a longing glance at the chocolate display and followed Angelo across the room, where she sat at the counter. He stood opposite her, reached below the varnished surface and brought out an elegant bottle of pale gold wine. The signature Tremiato label – golden clusters of cascading grapes, surrounding a Florentine "T" on a black background – dressed the bottle. Sadie waited politely while Angelo poured a half inch of chardonnay into her glass, and then brought it to her lips, tasting it and nodding her immediate approval. "Delicious," she exclaimed, taking another sip before setting the glass down.

"That is our best seller," Angelo said. "It's a good wine to have on hand – for unexpected company, or just to relax after a hard day. Just keep it chilled and enjoy with light appetizers or an entrée of salmon, perhaps."

"I could see serving it with a Gruyere fondue," Sadie said. "Or maybe halibut with a lemon-caper sauce."

"Ah, yes," Angelo said. "I see you know how to match a fine wine like this with a culinary compliment." He slid a basket of crackers next to Sadie's glass. "So what brings you to our winery?"

Sadie recognized the tone as polite small talk, as opposed to genuine interest, and answered accordingly. "I'm just taking a weekend away from the city, stopping here and there along Highway 29. There's so much to explore. I didn't even know where to start, so I just popped in here first."

"Well, you started at the right place," Angelo beamed. "We're one of the oldest wineries in the area. My great-grandfather Giovanni Tremiato started the business in 1897. He passed the business on to my grandfather, Angelo – I am named after him, you see. And Grandfather left it to my father, Gustavo, who just passed away last year."

"I'm so sorry for your loss," Sadie said. Angelo nodded courteously. "And you run it now?" Sadie asked, taking another sip of the Chardonnay.

"Yes, with my brother, Stefano."

"And his sister," a third voice added from behind Sadie. A woman with hazel eyes and dark brown hair swept up in a bun stood in the doorway, dressed in a plain navy blue dress and low pumps.

Angelo cleared his throat and flashed a wide grin that Sadie suspected lacked sincerity. "This is my sister, Luisa."

"Also one of the owners," Luisa clarified. She entered the room and took a place behind the counter next to her brother. She reached in front of Angelo with a kind of defiant confidence, lifted the bottle and added more wine to Sadie's glass.

"Thank you," Sadie said. The tension between the brother and sister was palpable. "I'm Sadie."

"Are you visiting from out of town?" Luisa had stepped back, but maintained a territorial stance.

Sadie nodded, her wine glass a few inches from her lips. "Yes, from San Francisco. I decided to take a break from the city for a few days, so I drove up here."

"I can see wanting to get out of the city," Angelo said. "I was just there for a trade show. I'm down there on business at least a couple times a month and that's more than enough, really. I prefer the tranquility of the wine country. And this is home to me."

"It's home to all members of the Tremiato family," Luisa added, as if she were correcting her brother.

"Do you have a large family? And do they all work at the winery?" Sadie hoped her questions sounded more casual than investigatory, though she waited eagerly for the answer. She already knew the family make-up from talks with Matteo, but wondered how the description would differ from the perspective of each of the other family members. She took a nonchalant sip of wine.

"Large is relative," Luisa said. "Sometimes we have a few too many working here, other times we could use a few more." Luisa grabbed an empty glass and poured an inch of wine for herself.

"There are three of us here, plus our mother," Angelo explained. "But we try to keep her from working too much. She's worked hard for many years, as did our father. Now it's our turn. From generation to generation, as family businesses go."

Sadie smiled, noticing Luisa did not correct Angelo on the number of siblings, which clearly excluded Matteo, who would have made four. Although Matteo had said he wasn't regarded as part of the family, to hear it from his own brother and sister seemed sad.

"Are you here for the weekend?" Angelo asked. "We have an event tomorrow, our annual Harvest Festival. Perhaps you can make it."

"Is it harvest time?" Sadie asked. "I'm afraid I don't know much about wine making."

"It's slightly past harvest time," Angelo said. "We're too busy to manage a festival during the actual harvest. We harvested our white wines last month, and we just finished with the reds. Now we can finally relax and celebrate the season. We want our employees to be able to enjoy the festival as much as our guests. In any case, I do hope you can make it."

"I might be able to," Sadie said. "I'm here for a couple of nights."

Angelo moved to offer Sadie more wine, but she shook her head. "No more, thank you. I should be going. I need to go get settled in somewhere, but I'll try to come back tomorrow."

"Are you staying in town?" Angelo picked up Sadie's wine glass and wiped down the counter.

Sadie nodded. "That's the plan. When I checked the internet this morning, it looked like there were quite a few vacancies, so I took a chance and just drove up without a reservation, played it by ear, as they say."

"You should stay at Tina's place," Angelo said, turning to Luisa. "Don't you think Tina has openings tonight? She had some people cancel earlier."

"I imagine she does," Luisa said. She eyed Sadie with little warmth and handed her a small brochure from behind the counter.

"Tina's place?" Sadie said, looking down at the pamphlet. The picture on the cover showed an exquisite Victorian bed and breakfast with immaculate landscaping and a sign over the door announcing it as "The Vintage Vine."

"Stefano's wife," Angelo explained. "Both my brother and sister-in-law, Tina, have a passion for business. They own The Vintage Vine, as well as Vines and Tines, a shop on the town plaza. Tina runs the bed and breakfast, while Stefano runs the store."

"And then we have the business here, of course," Luisa added. "Which we *all* run." The look she shot Angelo made it clear she felt some put in more effort than others, perhaps because their business energy was centered elsewhere.

"Angelo! Luisa!" The sharp voice caused Sadie to jump, as focused as she was on the stiff interaction between brother and sister. All three turned to face a short, stout woman with salt and pepper hair who stepped into the doorway. She noticed Sadie and smiled, revealing a gleaming gold cap on a front tooth. "*Scusi...*"

"Mama, we have a visitor, as you can see," Angelo said. "Sadie is here from San Francisco for the weekend. I think she might stay at Tina's place." He turned back to Sadie. "This is our mother, Elena Tremiato."

"Ah, excellent!" Elena shouted before Sadie could even say hello. "You will love our Tina's place. She has decorated it so beautifully! A princess could live there."

Sadie noticed Luisa turning away as Elena raved about Tina's wonderful bed and breakfast. Did she sense jealousy?

Sadie waved the brochure in the air with enthusiasm that matched Elena's. "I'll drive by the store and the inn. Thanks so much for the recommendation." Balancing her tote bag's straps delicately on her shoulder, she said goodbye and made her way to the parking lot as a heated exchange of words started up behind her. However pleasant the winery appeared on the surface, the undercurrents were as angry and tense as the phone call she'd overheard with Matteo. Something wasn't quite right at the Tremiato Winery. The question was: what was it?

CHAPTER THREE

Sadie hopped in the car, twisting the key in the ignition and checking her makeup in the visor's mirror at the same time. *Not enough eye shadow*, she mused. *Or maybe just a brighter shade...* She'd pick up a festive color when she had a chance.

"What do you think, Coco?" Sadie reached into the tote bag and pulled out the squirming ball of fluff, holding Coco up against her face so they could look in the mirror together. "C'mon, now, one yip for an exotic color around the eyes, two yips for brighter lipstick."

Instead of yipping an answer, the Yorkie gave Sadie's cheek a canine kiss. Sadie reciprocated with a pat on the head. "I know, Coco, you love me just as I am. I feel the same way. Besides, I don't think you'd care for lipstick unless it tasted like peanut butter." Sadie adjusted the velvet pillow in the tote bag, placed the dog back inside and adjusted the seatbelt harness that held the bag in place. "Let's go check out this inn of Tina's. What do you say to that?" She smiled at the immediate yip of approval. It was rare she didn't gain Coco's enthusiasm when the word "go" turned up anywhere in a sentence.

She flipped the visor up and clicked through the radio stations. She settled on jazz and cranked the volume up before she backed the car out of the parking spot. With the convertible top down and Coltrane blasting across the open vineyards, she cruised out to the main highway.

As she left the Tremiato property behind for magazine-perfect scenery, Sadie passed winery after winery with decorative entrances and fancy signage inviting visitors to meander up vineyard-flanked driveways. Dozens of businesses of all sizes with names of French, Italian or uncertain origin, all promised the same thing: California-grown wine from one of the world's most famous wine areas. She wished she had time to visit them all and compare!

The town center was hopping. Tourists bustled down sidewalks, chatting with each other and ducking in and out of boutiques. Sadie circled at least ten minutes before she found a parking place on a side street. Even that was a challenge; she parallel parked between two greedy vehicles that had left plenty of room on opposite ends, but little for her. Fortunately, the gentle taps she'd made on their bumpers while squeezing into the small space didn't leave any marks.

She found Vines and Tines wedged between a coffee house and a pet boutique. *A must visit! Maybe I'll find a sweet coat with a grapevine design for Coco.*

Vines and Tines' entrance, two stately doors made of walnut-framed stained glass, enchanted Sadie. She smiled as she reached for the door handles, over-sized and shaped like forks. Clever! Whimsical! If the interior proved to be just as charming, it would be worth visiting, whether it provided information or not.

Sadie assumed the handsome young man behind the cash register was Stefano. Two young women leaned against the counter fiddling with the impulse buy displays, whispering and batting their lashes. The tall, muscular man grinned and leaned toward the smitten customers. Ah, to be young again, Sadie thought. In years past, she might have fought for his attention herself. As it was, his preoccupation with the young women gave her a chance to observe. Or spy, to be more specific.

Vines and Tines carried such distinctive and whimsical merchandise that Sadie came close to forgetting the actual purpose of her visit. A sleek, teak table held a setting for an elegant, upscale dinner; a floral arrangement of ivory roses and bursts of dark red berries matched the silk placemats. An ornate silver wine holder encircled a bottle of Tremiato Pinot Noir, the rich color of the wine echoing the deep colors embedded in the centerpiece, almost as if the berries had been infused with the wine itself. Business cards from a local event planner formed a tiny fan on one corner of the table.

Instinctively, Sadie leaned forward to smell the flowers, realizing halfway there that her nose was likely to run into silk. To her surprise, the roses were real.

Another table displayed a picnic fit for a perfect summer day. This table was rustic and casual and, had it not been covered with the heavenly picnic fare, could have been an item in the back pages of any outdoor furniture magazine. But the woven basket overflowing with fruit, cheese and baguettes in the center of the table enticed guests to slide onto one of the redwood benches, cut a generous slice of Gouda from an apple-shaped serving board, and enjoy it with an imported English water cracker. Sadie guessed both the cheese and crackers were samples to be tasted. If the bottle of Tremiato Chardonnay on the table had been open, the situation would have been perfect.

Sadie had never been shy, so she set down her tote bag gently on one bench, scooted in beside it and gathered a generous serving of cheese and crackers onto a sturdy blue plate, knocking over two hand-painted acrylic wine glasses and a papier mâché watermelon in the process. A quiet "yip" escaped the tote, and Sadie hushed the unseen Coco, then shrugged her shoulders and smiled sweetly at the customers who had turned toward her. As the attention shifted away from her again, she broke a water cracker in half and slyly slipped it into her tote bag.

"Dishwasher and microwave safe!"

Even Stefano's voice was attractive, Sadie thought as she looked up at the second oldest Tremiato brother. She saw that his fan club had departed. She straightened up, pulled her tote bag a bit closer, and swallowed a mouthful of Brie.

"Those are great qualities for dishware to have." Sadie lifted her plate to offer him cheese and crackers but quickly set it down, realizing the ridiculousness of the move.

Stefano picked up a plate and tapped it with his finger, the blunt sound revealing the dish was plastic. "Durable and unbreakable," he added. "Perfect for a picnic. Just toss the dishes back in the basket after your meal and throw them in the dishwasher when you get home."

"Every household should have some!" Sadie said. She wondered if she'd just committed to buying a set of the blue picnic ware. "Speaking of home, I'm in need of one for the weekend. Angelo and Luisa recommended your wife's bed and breakfast. They thought there might be an opening tonight. They gave me a brochure."

"So you've been to our family vineyards." Stefano grinned. "And now our shop – my shop, that is. This business is independent of the winery, which is a family business. The Vintage Vine, our bed and breakfast, and this shop belong only to me and my wife, not to the Tremiato family. Let me call Tina to let her know to expect you."

Sadie watched Stefano walk away, curious about his comments. Sadie wondered why Stefano felt a need to point out that the businesses he and Tina ran did not exist under the umbrella of the Tremiato vineyards and winery. Was this out of pride? Or maybe he just had a possessive nature. Either way, it seemed an odd thing for him to have pointed out so emphatically. Why would he think she needed to know who owned the various businesses? Why would he be so eager to say?

Stefano soon returned looking cheerful and announced that he'd spoken with Tina and there was definitely a room available.

"You're in luck, my dear. There's just one room open, but it's a very nice one with a view of the back garden."

"That sounds perfect!" As Sadie stood, she reached for another slice of cheese. "I'd better go get checked in, before someone else books the room."

"Oh, don't worry," Stefano said. "Tina is holding it for you. Head down Main Street, take a left at the old courthouse, a right three blocks later on Baker, and then one more right on Spruce. The inn will be on the left. You can't miss it. There's a beautifully carved wood sign in front."

"I'll do just that, thank you," Sadie said. "I'm grateful for your exceptional hospitality, and for your brother and sister's kindness. Your family is most charming."

"Yes, I suppose they can be." Stefano's reply was aloof, as if he didn't agree with Sadie's assessment of his siblings.

Again, Sadie sensed tension within the family. This matched Matteo's tone during the phone call she'd overheard. She was more certain than ever that Matteo had been speaking with a family member – possibly this family member.

"I may just be back for that picnic ware," Sadie said as she exited, Stefano accompanying her. She bid him goodbye, headed to the car and drove off along Main Street.

One left and two right turns brought Sadie to The Vintage Vine. Not quite in the center of town, yet close enough to stroll to shops and cafes, the charming bed and breakfast was in a perfect location. Sadie compared the picture of the inn on the brochure to the building in front of her. The actual B&B was even more enchanting than its photograph. Miniature roses wove themselves through the white porch railings, and containers of primrose and pansies adorned the stairs. A stained glass window was built into the front door with smaller matching windows to each side of the wooden doorframe. A rocking chair faced inward from one side of the porch. The prospect of sipping chilled wine while rocking was soothing enough to draw Sadie from her car. She climbed the stairs to the front porch and knocked gently on the door.

Tina Tremiato was about 5'2" and not an ounce over 100 pounds, as far as Sadie could tell. Somehow she'd expected someone taller and more physically commanding, perhaps because Stefano seemed so large and powerful. Even as she thought this, she knew it was just another stereotype that comes from nowhere – the vision of what a couple would look like. Once the woman spoke, Sadie knew Tina was as tough as Stefano seemed to be. Despite her size, Tina Tremiato spoke boldly and with confidence. She was not to be underestimated.

"Good afternoon. You must be Sadie." The innkeeper's stance was friendly, yet alert, as if she were prepared to welcome customers, but not hesitant to shoo away solicitors.

"Yes, I'm Sadie Kramer. How did you know so certainly?"

Tina stepped back and ushered Sadie into an elegant parlor. "Stefano said you were the height of fashion, like a walking field of wildflowers."

Sadie laughed, thrilled that her fashion statement had made such an impression, then stood and took in everything she could see of the front of the inn.

"Oh my, what a gorgeous place you have!" Sadie exclaimed. "Every bit as beautiful as in the brochure." She pulled the pamphlet out of her tote bag's side pocket and waved it in the air. "I'm delighted you have a room available!"

"Yes, the Merlot Room is available tonight, because of a cancellation." Tina's voice trailed off as she moved to a registration desk and made a note in the ledger. "It's a lovely room with a queen bed and small sitting area. The private bath has a claw foot tub, and the room has a view of the back garden."

"Would it happen to be available for two nights?" Sadie watched as Tina flipped a page over and nodded.

"Absolutely."

"Perfect!" Sadie beamed.

"Ah, a weekend escape, I take it." Tina smiled as she handed Sadie a registration card and a pen.

"Yes, exactly!" Sadie filled out the required information and gave Tina a credit card to authorize the stay. With key in hand, she headed off to settle in.

She found the Merlot Room at the end of the main hall not far from a back door to the inn, a convenient spot for easy entrances and exits. Other than the possibility of slight noise from a side parking lot, the location promised to be fairly quiet since it was away from the common rooms where other guests might congregate over wine and cheese in the late afternoon or play cards or board games in the evening. She did play a mean game of Gin Rummy; if she had time, maybe she'd round up some players at some point during her visit.

One trip to the car was all it took to bring in what she needed – her overnight bag and a small, folding crate that she considered to be Coco's portable palace. She'd had it custom designed, along with a floral canvas bag that was large enough to hold the folded contraption and nondescript enough to pass as a small portfolio or flat case of some sort. After all, some establishments just didn't have a full appreciation of canine chicanery.

"What do you think, Coco? Should we set you up near the window?" Sadie leaned over the tote bag, which she'd placed on a comfy wing-backed chair. This could be a risky move since Coco sometimes batted a paw upwards whenever a hint of freedom was in the air. Fortunately, Coco weighed just four pounds, so even a swat on Sadie's nose would have done little damage.

Sadie set Coco's crate up near the window, pausing to note the beautifully landscaped back garden. A cobblestone pathway meandered from the inn's back door to the parking lot, passing clusters of purple iris and yellow daffodils. Cornflower blue agapanthus stood tall above a sea of Irish moss, a park-style bench nearby inviting guests to sit and relax a spell. Sadie made a note to herself to take advantage of that particular spot to enjoy a couple of chapters from her current mystery read.

It only took a few minutes to set up Coco's elegant accommodation. The light metal "palace" unfolded easily, its raw silk lining already attached to the interior. Sadie quickly placed the Yorkie's favorite toy – a petite stuffed octopus – in one corner, along with the tiny china bowls that served as food and water dishes. The Villeroy pattern actually matched the garden outside.

Once Coco was settled and content, Sadie unpacked a few clothes and checked her cell phone to find a message from Flair. She moved the empty tote bag onto the floor, slid into the wing-backed chair, and called the store. Her assistant manager answered the phone right away.

"Hi, Amber, everything fine at Flair?" Amber was a solid generation behind Sadie but had a natural knack for knowing what fashion styles people preferred, regardless of their ages. She had an uncanny memory that allowed her to remember the last few purchases a customer had made. In addition, she shared Sadie's love of chocolate, which was a plus in Sadie's book.

"Everything's fine," Amber said. "I just wanted you to know that new jewelry line came in, the one that goes well with the silk scarves we ordered at the last gift show. Do you want me to put those out and redo the display in the front window to include a few pieces?"

"Great idea," Sadie replied. "Just check the packing slip to make sure nothing's missing and then price each item before putting it out. Anything else?"

"Mrs. Gillespie picked up that beaded vest she special ordered…and, nothing else that I can think of. Oh, except, I tried to get some afternoon treats for customers from Matteo's today, but his shop was closed."

"That's odd," Sadie said. "He always stays open until six o'clock or later, since so many people stop by after work."

"I know, that's why it struck me as strange. His sign is turned to 'closed,' and there's no note to explain why."

"Thanks, Amber. I wouldn't worry about it. Maybe he wasn't feeling well and just closed up early. But you might check at noon tomorrow, when he usually opens."

"I will, Sadie. You just enjoy your weekend."

"I plan to!" Sadie wanted to share her enthusiasm with Amber. "I'm at an enchanting bed and breakfast and planning to attend a festival tomorrow. And St. Vin has some unique shops. I should be able to get some ideas for ours. Always good to find new things."

Sadie ended the call and set her phone on an antique oak dresser. She frowned. Between the argument she'd overheard Matteo having and now his closing the shop early, something was definitely not right.

CHAPTER FOUR

Sadie approached the Tremiato winery anticipating all the happy elements of a festival: a crowded parking lot, visitors sipping wine cheerfully and sampling other goodies in the tasting room, both edible and not. What she found, instead, was anything but a party. Several police cars, lights flashing, blocked a portion of the parking lot. She pulled up as far as possible, parked her car and walked closer. No one seemed to notice her arrival, which suited her just fine. She circled the area, joining a group of onlookers who held glasses with varying shades of white, rosé or red wine. A few took sips, while most simply clutched their drinks and stared.

"What happened?" Sadie asked a woman with a wide-brimmed hat shading a face with faint traces of wrinkles that marked her as middle-aged.

"Oh, it's terrible," the woman said, her voice trembling. "A body, can you believe it? And such a nice family. I can't believe it. I just can't believe it." She paused, turning to look at Sadie. "Can you believe it? Of course not. Who could?" She turned back to watch the activity, satisfied at her answer to her own question.

"Is it a family member?" Somehow it seemed more tragic if it turned out to be someone she'd met, a thought that struck her as slightly irrational.

"I don't know. The police won't let anyone near. They're questioning them one at a time." The woman gulped some red wine, splashing a few drops of it on her beige cable knit sweater as she removed the glass from her lips.

Sadie looked around. Angelo stood at the tasting room entrance, waving his arms as he carried on a heated discussion with an officer. The elderly mother, Elena, sat on a patio chair, wringing her hands and dabbing her eyes with a handkerchief, an impassive Luisa at her side, one hand resting on her mother's shoulder.

Not a family member, Sadie thought, seeing how unmoved Luisa was by the turn of events. A work hand, perhaps? Or simply a visitor? Sadie shuddered at the last thought. Wrong place, wrong time. After all, she was a visitor and might very well have been the victim.

Circling the crowd, she worked her way closer to Angelo and the police officer, moving close enough to hear part, though not all, of the animated discussion.

"I don't even know what he was doing here," Angelo shouted at the officer questioning him. "We stopped meeting with him weeks ago."

Sadie watched the officer pose another question, his hushed words impossible to hear. It was clear he was trying to get the agitated Tremiato brother to calm down by speaking softly. Angelo ran one hand through his hair and began to pace. "None of this makes any sense."

"I think that's enough," a voice interrupted.

Sadie looked over her shoulder, watching Luisa approach. Just as Luisa began to speak with Angelo and the officer, a loud scream from the fermentation building shattered her efforts.

"No! Please, this is some crazy mistake!" Two deputies exited the building, escorting out a distraught woman. Sadie gasped. It was Tina Tremiato, owner of The Vintage Vine. Stefano was nowhere in sight. Elena walked to Tina, handkerchief flouncing in the air as she shook her hand at the deputies.

"Enough! You will let my son's wife go right now." Elena attempted to pull Tina toward her, but the deputies stopped her.

"I'm sorry, ma'am. But we need to take her in for questioning."

Interesting that Stefano was not with Tina at such a time of crisis, Sadie mused. Probably at the store, or on his way. As if on cue, a car pulled up alongside the building. Stefano jumped out of the vehicle.

"Questioning? At a time like this?" Luisa's stern tone caused the deputies to glance at each other and then back to her as one deputy replied.

"Yes, precisely at a time like this. She's the one who discovered the body. We need to get details while they're fresh in her mind."

Not to mention finding out if she's responsible, Sadie added silently.

"That's ridiculous!" Stefano shouted as he arrived at Tina's side.

"Sir, please lower your voice." The deputy attempted to move Tina along, but Stefano blocked the way.

"Sir, I'll need you to step aside. You're welcome to meet us at the station."

Luisa stepped forward and placed a hand on Stefano's arm, much in the same reassuring way that she'd touched their mother's shoulder before.

"It's OK, Stefano. We'll call Nick and he'll straighten this out in no time."

Stefano turned to Luisa. "How can you be so calm? This is our family, our business, our reputation. You can't trust that a lawyer can solve everything. Nick is a nice guy, but don't forget lawyers are ultimately after that paycheck."

"You just don't approve of me dating him," Luisa said, her voice cool.

"I've never said that."

"You don't have to, Stefano. I know you."

Sadie watched as the deputies skirted the arguing siblings and escorted Tina to a police car. It struck Sadie as odd that instead of following closely behind the officers and Tina, Stefano continued to argue with Luisa. In fact, all the interactions between the Tremiatos seemed fraught with tension and criticism. How the family managed to run a business – several businesses – without imploding was a puzzle. That phone call she'd overheard at the chocolate store certainly fit into the family dynamics she'd observed since she arrived at the winery. Yet Matteo was supposedly estranged from the family. Or was he?

"*Basta!*" Elena's command stopped the arguing between Stefano and Luisa. "That is enough! We will not talk more here. There are guests and *polizia!*"

Like obedient children, the two quieted down.

"That man should not have been here," Elena continued, waving her handkerchief again. "I told him he'd be sorry if he came around again!"

Luisa hurried to hush her mother. "Shhh. Stop talking!"

"He pushed too hard, Luisa," Elena continued. "It was insulting, as if I'm not capable of handling our family business myself!"

"Mama," Luisa said, "Let me take you to the house to rest. You're upset and not thinking clearly."

Luisa took Elena to the farmhouse behind the tasting room, to settle her in the family's living quarters. Stefano returned to his car, started it up and followed the squad car holding Tina as it wound its way down the driveway. Sadie watched as the police secured the fermentation building with yellow tape and stood by, probably waiting for the coroner. Most guests returned to their cars, anxious to get away from the unpleasant scene. A few chose to calm their nerves with another glass or two of wine in the tasting room.

Sadie weighed her options and decided to head to the tasting room. A glass of chardonnay didn't sound too bad after the scene she'd just witnessed. And she had a hunch there were clues all around her that could tell her what was happening with the Tremiato family. Whatever was going on at the property was surely connected to Matteo's argument on the phone. Hadn't Matteo told the person on the other end of the line to stop threatening him? Sadie shuddered. No, she wouldn't entertain those kinds of thoughts. She'd been friends with Matteo for years.

The tasting room was buzzing like a beehive, the guests who'd chosen to stay chatting up a storm. Angelo was busy pouring half glasses of wine, but seemed tight-lipped. His gaze flitted from one guest to the next, to the front door, the back door and back to the guests. Sadie thought he looked a cross between lost and nervous, yet not 100 percent one way or the other. Was he watching for someone in particular?

Sadie bustled through the small crowd and leaned against the counter, grabbing a miniature crab cake off one of many trays intended to feed a much larger group than remained. She was in the process of reaching for a second when she saw Luisa step up beside Angelo and whisper to him. Angelo set the wine bottle down and stepped aside, clearing a few glasses guests had left after the commotion began.

"Ladies and gentlemen," Luisa said. "As you know we've had a terrible shock today. I'm so sorry you had to be here for this tragedy when you expected a happy celebration. I'm afraid we need to postpone the festival to next weekend. If you're on our mailing list, you'll receive a reminder. If you aren't, please sign up. The mailing list forms are by the front door." She paused to allow a few seconds of polite, but nervous laughter. "Thank you for understanding. We hope to see you all next week."

The small crowd took the immediate hint, most setting their glasses down and heading for the door. A few took generous swigs of wine before they followed the other guests. The woman with the wide-brimmed hat, who had lingered with the others, grabbed a slice of bruschetta on her way out. *How insensitive*, Sadie thought, then paused. *Or just practical?* She grabbed a bruschetta for herself and headed for the door.

"Excuse me!"

Sadie recognized Luisa's voice and her inner third grader prepared to say, "She took one first!" However, she held her tongue, turned around and returned to the counter.

"We met yesterday, I think." Luisa didn't make eye contact, instead surveying the full trays that spanned the length of the counter.

"Yes," Sadie said. "I came back for the event today, but it's clearly a bad time, so I'll go and let your family have privacy."

"That's nice of you," Luisa said, her tone noncommittal. "I was wondering if you happen to be staying at my sister-in-law's bed and breakfast, The Vintage Vine, the inn we recommended to you yesterday."

Sadie paused searching for the right words. After all, they'd just watched the police cart off the innkeeper. "Well, I am, but perhaps I should look for another room, in view of the circumstances." The thought hadn't occurred to her yet, but it might not be the best lodging choice for the evening. The police might need to search the place, and what would guests do without an innkeeper? Would other guests even be staying? Did Tina have an assistant to take over?

"I'm glad you're a guest there," Luisa said, ignoring Sadie's statement about possibly changing inns. "We can't possibly eat all this food we had catered in. I need to stay with our mother, who's very upset, and Angelo is going to be tied up at the fermentation building with police reports and who knows what other paperwork. I was wondering if you might take at least some of this back with you. At least there's a full house, so it won't go to waste."

Sadie eyed a tray of stuffed mushrooms. "Of course, anything to help." *Where was the chocolate?*

"Thank you. How many can you take?"

"Three." Sadie paused, thinking. "No, I could take four, I think." *The tote bag can go on the floor. Coco won't mind.*

Luisa stepped into a back room and brought out foil to cover the trays. She dropped the foil on the counter, telling Sadie to pick a variety, then pulled a cell phone out of a cobalt blue Coach bag and returned to the back room. Sadie tried to listen in – eavesdropping being a necessary evil in her side career – but the conversation was too hushed, and

Luisa's voice maintained its usual calm. Sadie couldn't help but wonder if this monotone manner indicated that Luisa was less than satisfied with the family business, or even the family itself.

Choosing one tray each of bruschetta, stuffed mushrooms, an array of cheese and a carefully selected mixture of miniature quiches and crab cakes, Sadie covered the fancy food with foil and waited for Luisa to return. The phone call ended, but Luisa didn't emerge from the back, so Sadie took a tray to the car, setting her tote bag on the floor to make room for the others. After three more trips, she was done. She returned once more to tell Luisa she was leaving, but the tasting room was still empty. An additional box was on the counter with a note attached in perfect cursive saying, "Take this, too, please."

"Luisa?" Sadie's call to the sole Tremiato daughter went unanswered. "I'm leaving now." Again, no response, though this gave her time to peek inside the box. *Chocolate-drizzled cream puffs!*

After one last attempt to tell Luisa she was leaving, Sadie loaded the dessert box into her car. A glance toward the police tape showed her the coroner had arrived in a county ambulance. Happy to skip the next round of activity – she'd never been too crazy about body bags – Sadie buckled up and headed back to The Vintage Vine, exquisite feast in tow.

CHAPTER FIVE

Sadie arrived back at The Vintage Vine to find two police cars already parked in front. The lack of flashing lights and yellow police tape only took a slight edge off the scene. Somehow she'd expected to return to a quiet inn and had wondered what to explain or not explain to other guests. Now that problem was solved. Maybe. Of course the police had sent cars already! Why hadn't that occurred to her? If they were considering Tina a suspect, they'd want to gather any evidence before it could be disturbed. Or if they believed someone else to be involved, they'd still need to search the inn before anything incriminating could disappear.

Parking her car in the side lot, Sadie grabbed her tote bag and one tray and entered through the back door. She dropped her tote bag off in her room and took the tray to the kitchen, where she found two officers searching drawers.

"Ma'am, you'll need to stay out of here until we finish searching the kitchen."

"I understand," Sadie said. "I'm just not sure where to put these trays then. I have three more in the car."

One officer paused, the beam from a flashlight lingering inside a cupboard. "What's in them?"

"Appetizers from the Harvest Festival. It's been postponed because...well, for obvious reasons, and the Tremiatos didn't want all that food to go to waste."

The two officers exchanged glances. "Go ahead and put them on the center island," one said.

"Yes, we may need to search those, too," the other added. "Depends what they are, right, officer?" He looked at his partner with a hint of a smile.

"Crab cakes, bruschetta, stuffed mushrooms and miniature quiches," Sadie said, watching their eyes widen. "And some chocolate drizzled cream puffs." *Though I should be keeping those myself.*

"Oh, yes," the second officer said, not even hiding his grin. "We'll definitely need to search those."

Sadie returned the grin and set the tray down. "Thank you, officers. I like it when law enforcement does a thorough job."

"We do our best." "We aim to please." The men spoke over each other.

Sadie made three trips to her car, bringing in the trays one at a time. Each time, she glanced around, trying to determine if the officers had found anything of interest. It didn't appear so, though someone had definitely lifted the foil cover on the bruschetta tray. She returned to her room, transferred Coco from tote to palace, and sat down, looking out at the garden.

Several questions gnawed at her. Who was the victim? She'd overheard Elena Tremiato say she'd told the victim he'd be sorry if he kept coming around. That certainly didn't look good for Elena. But an elderly mother wouldn't be capable of a crime like that, would she?

Sadie glanced at the clock on the nightstand. Almost noon. Flair would be opening in a few minutes. She pulled her cell phone out of the tote bag's side pocket and called the boutique. Amber answered on the first ring.

"Good morning! Thank you for calling Flair! Fashion at your fingertips!"

"Amber, how much coffee have you had this morning?"

A few seconds of silence preceded the answer. "A double espresso at Jay's Java Joint on the way here."

"And?"

"Two cups of dark French roast in the back office." A pause. "OK, three."

"You know where the decaf is, in the cupboard? Make yourself a pot."

"Roger that. Wait a sec, let me open up."

Sadie waited as Amber put the phone down with an enthusiastic smack on the counter and clicked her heels across the boutique's floor. After a jingle of bells that signaled the swing of the front door, Amber returned to the phone.

"OK, open for another day of business. No customers yet."

"How about Matteo's shop?" Sadie could swear she heard a muffled slurp of a beverage.

"It didn't look open to me," Amber said. "Let me check." Again the phone hit the counter and the heels clattered across the floor. When Amber came back, Sadie heard the answer she'd feared.

"Closed. Sorry, Sadie. I'm sure you're worried about him."

"Well, now I really am," Sadie said, gathering her thoughts. "In all the years I've known him, I've never once seen Matteo open late. Or close early, for that matter. I'd hoped he'd just left to run an errand yesterday, but it sounds like something's up." Though she couldn't fathom the thought that Matteo could be involved with a murder, there was no question his absence was disturbing. Whether or not his absence had anything specifically to do with the events at the winery, the timing couldn't be coincidence. Perhaps Matteo was in trouble. Or worse? Sadie shuddered.

A jangling of bells in the background told Sadie that customers had entered. She asked Amber to call her when Matteo showed up and hung up.

"I am worried, Coco." Sadie smiled when the Yorkie yipped her response. "I knew you would be, too. You're also fond of Matteo, what with all those doggie treats he keeps on hand." Another yip.

"Ah, I know better than to say the word 'treat' out loud around you!" Sadie pulled a plastic bag from her suitcase, told Coco to sit, and rewarded her with a petite dog bone.

As Coco began to focus on decimating the treat, Sadie heard voices somewhere in the inn. She left her happy dog and followed the murmuring until she arrived at a gathering of guests in the front parlor. Instead of the cheerful exchanges and animated card games from the previous evening, she found a group of nervous people whispering their fears. Shock was a common theme.

"Did you hear?" A man with frizzy hair and a chin that was far too pointy looked at Sadie through wire-rimmed spectacles. She had to force herself to focus on his words instead of staring at his lavender, paisley printed shirt, which gave his face the pallor of a skinned potato. "There was a murder in town and the innkeeper has been arrested."

The others echoed him fretfully. The sounds of the officers continuing to search the premises did nothing to relieve the guests' fears.

"Yes, I'm aware of that," Sadie said. "But let's not jump to conclusions. Just because she was taken in for questioning doesn't mean she's guilty."

"Well, I heard she was found at the murder scene," a woman said. "That sounds suspicious to me."

"That's not how things work," Sadie said. "Suspicious and guilty are two different things. I was at the winery when the police picked her up, and she looked distraught, not guilty."

"You were there?" several guests asked simultaneously.

"Yes, I was. The innkeeper's family owns the Tremiato Winery. You'll see their brochures in the lobby. In any case, family had – or planned to have – a Harvest Festival today, which is why I was there. It's now been postponed, for obvious reasons."

"Well, I'm not staying here," a woman said. "This is way too creepy. I mean, anyone could be next."

"I assure you, that's not going to happen," a deep voice said. Sadie turned toward the parlor's doorway to see Stefano had entered. He looked haggard, but more composed than he had earlier. *Not that anyone could be expected to look composed while watching a spouse being dragged away by law enforcement,* Sadie thought.

"Tina will be back in a few hours. This is all a big misunderstanding." He paused, looking around the room at the confused faces. "I'm Stefano, Tina's husband, and my wife and I own The Vintage Vines together, though she is the face of the B&B. Of course you may leave if you feel more comfortable doing so. We'll refund your lodging deposits, in view of the current circumstances, but I hope you'll stay."

With that, Stefano left the room to converse with the police, who had moved from the kitchen to the innkeepers' quarters. Guests split in different directions, some to their rooms and others out to explore the town. A few announced they were going to pack and leave, despite Stefano's assurances that they were safe.

Sadie followed Stefano as far as the kitchen, lingering by the center island with both cream puffs and eavesdropping in mind. The voices from the innkeeper quarters, a back area off the kitchen, were muffled. Still, she caught a few sentences as she pretended to rearrange the appetizers.

"No, nothing appears to be missing." Stefano sounded a tad abrupt and defensive to Sadie, as if he wanted to get the questions over with and see the officers on their way. Probably normal under the circumstances?

Sadie couldn't make out a question one officer posed, but heard Stefano's reply loud and clear. "Of course we haven't received any threats or seen any unusual activity! Don't you think we would have reported something like that?" *Yep, defensive. But why?*

"Settle down, Mr. Tremiato. We're just doing our job." A half-hearted apology followed this statement. Stefano walked back into the kitchen and noticed Sadie.

"You were at the store yesterday. And at the winery before that."

"Guilty as charged," Sadie quipped, immediately regretting her choice of words.

"Well, you certainly picked an interesting time to get acquainted with our family." Stefano looked under the foil covering one of the trays. "Ah, I see my sister dropped off food from the festival."

"Actually, she asked me to bring it back here, so she could stay and watch your mother."

"Oh! Of course! There's nothing Luisa likes more than taking care of everyone around her. Good old Luisa."

The sarcastic tone in Stefano's voice made it clear he was not his sister's greatest fan. In fact, Sadie was beginning to wonder if Luisa *had* fans. Was it because of her aloof – dare she say *cold fish* – personality, or was there more going on behind the scenes?

"Mr. Tremiato?" Both Sadie and Stefano turned to see an officer in the doorway, holding a radio in his hand. "You're welcome to pick your wife up at the station. They're done questioning her."

"She's not being charged?" Stefano sounded both relieved and surprised.

"No, sir. She's free to go."

"And so are we," the other officer said, joining the first. "We're just taking a few items to inspect. We'll return them as soon as possible."

"I'm following them," Stefano said. "Could you see if any of this will fit in the refrigerator? Just until Tina gets back here. I apologize for asking. I know you're a guest."

"I'm tickled pink to help," Sadie said. *Just one cream puff…*

Sadie watched Stefano disappear through the front door just behind the officers, who took a laptop and several plastic bags of possible evidence. Although it was impossible to tell exactly what each bag contained, she could have sworn one bag held bruschetta.

CHAPTER SIX

The evening flowed along without major incident. Celia, a part-time innkeeper with a willowy figure and shoulder-length brown curls, had set out wine and appetizers for the guests who had stayed. Talk tiptoed around the tragedy as everyone tried to pretend the day had turned normal. Even a few card games broke out, though the players were subdued.

Although Sadie normally loved cocktail hours for the camaraderie and chance to dig into the mysteries of her fellow human beings, her mind was too full of questions about the murder on the Tremiatos' property and the tension she sensed among the family members. After a half-hearted-attempt to get interested in a game of Spades, Sadie had feigned a headache and left to take Coco for a long walk around the neighborhood. She went to bed, exhausted from her mental gymnastics, and dreamed about the multiple nuances between the siblings that created a complicated puzzle.

The faint sound of crying awakened Sadie from her light, edgy sleep. She had a hunch the puzzle was about to get more complicated.

She slipped out to the parlor, but found it empty; so was the kitchen. She pulled her silk, chartreuse and lavender robe tighter around her. The sniffling sound was fainter than it had been in her room. As she retraced her steps, the muffled crying grew louder. Finally she cracked open the back door, just beyond her room. A safety light filtered across the yard and revealed Tina sitting on a bench behind the innkeeper quarters.

"Are you OK?"

Tina jumped as Sadie approached and tried to hide a crumpled tissue in one hand. Sadie felt a twinge for invading Tina's privacy, but subtlety was not one of her strengths, and she believed she could both offer some comfort and dig up some information at the same time.

"I'm fine," Tina said, though her voice quivered.

"If you need to talk, I'm a good listener." Usually, this was true, but the many unanswered questions might make it hard to focus, especially since one of those questions concerned Matteo's continued absence. Amber had called that evening to tell Sadie the chocolatier hadn't opened his store at all that day.

Suddenly, Tina said, "Look, Sadie, I know you and Matteo are friends." She swiped the sodden tissue under her eyes.

Sadie startled, feeling guilty for coming to town under false pretenses, though they weren't entirely false. She was due a weekend off, and she just managed to combine this mini-vacation with a little detective work. In any case, ending up in the middle of a murder had never been part of her plan. Cautiously, she sat next to Tina.

"Yes, we are friends. And I'm sorry I didn't say so right away. Matteo seemed agitated the day before I left, and I suspected it had to do with his family. I was worried. We've been friends for a long time, and I'd never seen him like that."

Tina reached over and patted Sadie's arm, a gesture designed to be friendly but that Sadie found a bit alarming. *The police let her go, but….* Instinctively, Sadie pulled her arm back a bit, then apologized.

"Don't worry," Tina sniffled, recognizing Sadie's unease. "I'm surprised the police let me go. After all, I was the one to discover…" She broke down crying before she could finish the sentence. "He was just there, you know? Sprawled out on the floor, surrounded by broken glass and red...liquid – blood, wine, both, I guess. And his neck...." She turned to Sadie, who simply nodded.

"Don't feel you have to talk, Tina. You've been through a lot. If you need to be alone, I can go back to my room."

"No, I want you to stay. I have to talk to someone. Matteo has always said you're a good person." She made a sound that was a cross between tears and a laugh. "And an exceptional customer."

Sadie laughed, too. "Yes, that's true. I can't get through an afternoon without a few of his truffles."

"Same here," Tina said. "He sneaks shipments up here, with false labels so his wacko family won't realize who sent them."

"I thought he wasn't in touch with any of your family."

"Ha," Tina replied. "Don't include me in that group of lunatics. I just married into the family. I had no idea I was getting into a dysfunctional mess."

"You can't talk to Stefano?"

Tina shook her head. "I'd have to see him to talk to him. He's always at the store. Or so he says. Sometimes I don't care that he's not around. His absence keeps the constant family drama away."

Tina lapsed into silence and then sighed. "I didn't do it, you know."

"Of course not," Sadie said. *That's what they all say...*

"But you're right about Matteo being estranged from the family," Tina continued. "The Tremiatos felt he disgraced them because he didn't take over the family business. And for chocolate? They see that as a silly hobby, not a career."

"They might take it seriously if they saw the lines of customers at his place," Sadie interjected.

"I know. He's very successful, and he's doing what he loves." Tina dabbed the tissue at her eyes, still fighting back tears. "But that means nothing to the Tremiatos. To them, it's about family pride. That winery is their whole life. Every family member is expected to carry equal weight."

"Yet Stefano has his own store."

"*Our* store," Tina clarified. "We own it together, though I have no desire to go there lately to watch his groupies hang around the counter. As for your point, Stefano sells massive amounts of Tremiato wine, holds tastings, displays the bottles in the windows. So he's still in the family's good graces though he works elsewhere. The store is the perfect feeder for winery visits, too. He recommends it to everyone and keeps brochures and maps on the counter."

"And you have the bed and breakfast to run."

"Yes, thank goodness. It gives me an excuse to stay away from all that craziness. Besides, I enjoy it. I was sorry to miss the wine and cheese hour today, but I was in no shape to be out there with guests. I'm lucky I have Celia to help out."

"She did a good job," Sadie said. "And it didn't hurt to have all those appetizers that Luisa sent over."

"Ah, yes, Luisa. She's an interesting one," Tina said, a tinge of sarcasm under the sniffles.

When she failed to elaborate, Sadie nudged her on. "How so?"

"You never quite know what's going on with her. If you try to get close, she backs away. She's fiercely proud of being a Tremiato, but as the only daughter she's at a disadvantage. With Matteo away, she's the oldest, yet Angelo makes most of the decisions about winery concerns. Luisa resents that."

"The plight of women in the business world."

"Exactly. And family politics combined with Old Italian traditions make it worse."

Sadie hesitated before posing her next question, but decided to go ahead.

"Tina, have you talked to Matteo today? Or last night"

Tina paused. "Not today, but I did talk to him last night. Wait, that's not right. It was yesterday afternoon, because I was still preparing the cheese tray for the guests, to set out with wine at 5. So I'd say it was 4:30 or so."

"How did he sound?" In order to not seem too nosy, Sadie added, "He seemed upset the day before, at his shop."

"That's odd," Tina said. "He sounded fine to me when he called yesterday. But there was a lot of noise in the background. We didn't talk long. I figured his store was extra busy. Or that he'd taken his cell phone out front, around customers. Though, come to think of it, that's odd, too. He always likes to keep his personal life separate from his business life."

"I don't think he called you from the store," Sadie ventured, knowing she was about to add to Tina's already heavy load of worries.

"Why do you say that?"

"Because, according to Amber, my assistant, he closed up shop early yesterday."

"Early? He never closes early! That shop is his life."

"It gets a little worse, I'm afraid. He didn't open up today at all."

Although it was too dark to see, Sadie imagined that Tina's face paled.

"No! This isn't good! This isn't good at all!" Tina stood up and started to walk away. "You have to excuse me."

"Tina? Tina?" Sadie's calls were to no avail. Tina had reached the back door and slipped inside the inn. The conversation was over.

CHAPTER SEVEN

"What do you make of this, Coco?"

The petite ball of fluff tipped her head to one side in curiosity as Sadie held the newspaper up, turning it in Coco's direction.

"It says here 'the coroner's office has identified the body found at the Tremiato Winery yesterday as 54-year-old Simon J. Flanagan, originally of Boston, Mass. Mr. Flanagan was an employee of Serrano-Flanagan, a Sacramento company in which he owned a small share of stock. He leaves behind a wife of 28 years and two grown children. Police are investigating the death as a homicide.'"

Coco responded by licking her paw and staying silent. Sadie pondered the news out loud. "Why would the dead body of a man from Sacramento be in the Tremiato fermentation building – apologies, Coco, that does sound a bit gross. Did his firm have business in this area?"

Sadie kicked off her leopard print slippers, fluffed the bed pillows and settled back against them to continue reading.

"'Serrano-Flanagan recently made a bid to purchase the Tremiato Winery, an offer that was refused by the fourth-generation vintners after considerable disagreement between family members.' Aha, Coco! I think we're getting somewhere. 'No further negotiations are known to have occurred since family turned down the bid. It is unknown whether or not the discovery of the victim at the Tremiato Winery is related to the attempt to buy the property and business. The family has not issued a statement at this time, and a call to the Tremiato family lawyer, Nick Perry, has not been returned."

Tossing the paper aside, Sadie mulled over the new information. Matteo had never mentioned anything about a bid to purchase the winery, though he rarely said anything about the family business at all. The newspaper article noted dissension amongst family members before the offer was rejected. Had Matteo been in on that? Just because he chose to stay away from family affairs didn't mean all family members stayed away from him. Case in point: the phone call she'd overheard at Matteo's shop. That could easily have been one of the siblings. And Tina, though not family by blood, was still a Tremiato and seemed to communicate with Matteo regularly.

"Curiouser and curiouser, Coco." The Yorkie shifted position and blinked.

Sadie sat up and took a sip of the coffee she'd found in the front room. She'd also grabbed a blueberry muffin. No other guests had been up and about to interrupt her interrogatory momentum, an advantage to being an early bird.

Choosing bright purple slacks and a white tunic with polka dots in various shades of lavender, Sadie wrapped a yellow scarf around her head and tied it at the side of her neck. She added chunky white earrings and a long strand of colorful glass baubles. Sliding into a pair of beaded flats, she refilled Coco's water dish, grabbed her cell phone, and went looking for Tina. She found the innkeeper restocking the breakfast buffet.

"Good morning," Sadie said. "Delicious blueberry muffins. I swiped one earlier, with a cup of coffee."

"Good morning, Sadie," Tina said as she set a bowl of fresh blackberries alongside a platter of honeydew melon. "I want to thank you for being such a good listener last night. I should never have imposed on you that way."

"Don't be silly!" Sadie exclaimed. "For one thing, I'm the one who asked you if you wanted to talk. And, besides, we all need to vent a little now and then. Plus we were both worried about Matteo. Speaking of which, have you been able to reach him?"

"No, but I'm not as worried now. I reached a friend of his, who told me Matteo had been talking about needing a break. He'd asked about borrowing fishing gear from the guy's back porch. When the friend checked last night, the gear was gone."

"So you think he went fishing?"

"It certainly sounds like it, don't you think?" Tina said. "Asking ahead of time for the gear? Seems clear cut to me."

Sadie nodded, but said nothing. *Maybe, maybe not. Seems a bit too convenient.*

"You're probably right," Sadie said, and hoped Tina didn't sense her doubts. She reached for another muffin and then stopped herself. A nice lunch in town a few hours later sounded appealing, and there was no point in spoiling her appetite by overeating now. "By the way, I'm thinking about staying another night, if the room isn't booked." *Things are far too interesting to leave now.*

"I'll check the registration book, but I'm sure that's fine. Sundays are quiet since people tend to head back home to prepare for work on Monday."

Tina finished rearranging pitchers of orange, apple and cranberry juice and moved to the front entryway. She glanced through registration records and nodded her head. "Yes, there's plenty of space. In fact, you can just keep the Merlot room."

"Perfect," Sadie said. "A calmer day in this lovely area would do me some good. Yesterday was hectic, to say the least." She paused. "Oh! I'm sorry! I shouldn't complain, considering what you've been through."

Tina waved her hand in the air, dismissing Sadie's concerns. "Don't worry. Obviously it wasn't an ideal situation for a weekend escape."

Not "an ideal situation?" Could there be any more of an understatement than that?

Sadie realized that mentioning the newspaper coverage of the murder to Tina might be insensitive, but she decided she would make the most of the innkeeper's current composure and began asking careful questions.

"I noticed the local paper had some coverage of the events at the winery yesterday." Sadie watched Tina, trying to gauge her reaction. Tina moved back into the breakfast room and shrugged her shoulders.

"I haven't had a chance to read it yet."

Somehow Sadie doubted this was true.

"Well, it identified the victim. Apparently, he had some business dealings with the winery recently." Sadie waited for a response while Tina circled the room, picking up a few small plates and coffee mugs that guests had left.

"You're talking about the proposed sale that didn't go through. You'll have to ask Stefano and Angelo about that. I have nothing to do with the business of the company."

Sadie flashed back to the sense of ownership that Angelo had shown when Sadie first entered the tasting room. At least until Luisa set him straight.

"Maybe I'll ask one of them," Sadie said. "I was thinking I'd go by the winery today, since I'm staying another night. If it's open today, that is."

"Oh, it'll certainly be open. In fact, it might even be busy. You know how gruesome people can be, chasing crime stories. Then again, maybe they'll be scared away." Tina paused. "Sadie, I'm barely holding it together. Do you mind if we drop this topic?"

"Of course. I apologize. I know this must be terribly hard for you. I'll stop by the winery, then," Sadie said. "I hope things get back to normal."

"You should consider coming back for the festival. Check with Angelo for the details when you go by the winery."

Or with Luisa, Sadie thought. Luisa seemed to be calling the shots regarding the festival, but Sadie assumed from Tina's comments about her sister-in-law the previous night that Luisa was unlikely to get credit for her hard work. Even unspoken, the tension between the women was obvious. And what was that all about, anyway?

Sadie returned to her room and gathered up Coco. She took her for a brief walk around the back garden before loading both herself and the petite canine in the car. Coco settled immediately into the soft velvet inside the tote bag, while Sadie buckled her seatbelt and pulled out onto the highway. Coco was a great travel dog, lulled to sleep by any movement of cars, trains or planes. This was indeed fortunate, as Sadie often headed off in one direction or another. Occasionally, she left Coco at home when she traveled. Amber took good care of her and customers enjoyed seeing her in the store. But, more often than not, Sadie took her along for company. Plus, Coco was like a living, breathing accessory, elegant and fluffy, perfect for any of Sadie's colorful outfits.

"So, Coco, what do you think of all this?" Sadie directed the question to the tote bag, glancing at it briefly and then quickly looking back at the road. It occurred to her that the driver of a car to her right probably thought she was talking to an empty seat, or perhaps to herself. Not that it should look that strange in this day and age of hands-off cell phone devices.

"I absolutely agree," Sadie said, answering her own question, having not received so much as a yip in reply. "Tina seems unusually calm this morning, all sorts of odd interactions are taking place between members of the Tremiato family, and I don't believe for a second that Matteo went fishing. So what do you think is going on?"

One glance up the driveway of the Tremiato Winery validated the theory that people were inclined to follow news stories. The parking lot was more than half full, with some visitors gawking at the fermentation building, which had been roped off the previous morning, while others, presumably, were in the tasting room. Sadie pulled into an open parking spot and headed inside, tote bag swaying from her arm.

Angelo was busy pouring two glasses of wine for a young couple at the counter. They had the rosy expressions of honeymooners, not an unusual sight in the wine country. It was a perfect area for a newlywed escape, flush with upscale inns, fine dining and pastoral vineyard scenes in every direction.

Sadie browsed the display shelves, eyeing the same tempting chocolate she'd seen on her first visit, then settled in at one end of the tasting counter. With a dozen other visitors milling around and Angelo occupied with the young couple, she took advantage of the time to look around.

The tourists in the tasting room seemed interested only in wine and small talk, not murder. Through her eavesdropping skills, she caught comments about vacation plans and the various wines they'd tried in the area. A few dropped names of other wineries nearby. Others bragged about the great deals they'd gotten on exquisite accommodations. Sadie suspected the lookie-loos who were following the crime news were all outside.

Luisa was nowhere to be seen. This hit Sadie as peculiar since Luisa had been so territorial the first day Sadie met her. Sadie finally caught sight of her through the open back door, which allowed a clear view across the yard to the family farmhouse. There, she watched as Luisa paced the front porch, stopped periodically to exchange words with Elena, who retorted by waving her arms and, though Sadie couldn't hear, spouting some undoubtedly sharp words. What were they arguing about? Luisa had specifically sent the appetizers off with Sadie the day before so that she could stay with Elena and comfort her. But there was nothing that looked comfortable about the discussion taking place now. Both women were upset.

If only I could hear them from here. Sadie stepped away from the counter and was about to head outside when the sound of Angelo's voice stopped her.

"Sadie, right? Here to taste our chardonnay again?"

"Absolutely," Sadie said, turning back toward the counter. "I was hoping to, but didn't want to interrupt you when you have other customers."

Angelo brought a glass out from behind the counter and poured a half inch of the winery's famed chardonnay. Sadie lifted the glass to her lips, stuck her nose in the rim to sniff it – after all, she'd seen experts do that on television – and took a sip, noticing that Angelo looked beyond her and out toward the farmhouse. A light crease crossed his forehead, disappearing instantly when Sadie set the glass down and looked up at him.

"I was here yesterday for the festival," Sadie ventured, "I'm sorry for what your family is going through. Plus all your visitors…You seemed so excited about the harvest celebration your winery was planning."

"Today is a new day. Yesterday was unfortunate, but it's over." Angelo tilted the bottle of wine over Sadie's glass, but she shook her head to turn down the refill.

"We've already rescheduled the festival for next weekend," Angelo continued.

"Well, good," Sadie said, wondering why Angelo spoke with the same nonchalance that Tina seemed to acquire overnight. That cool attitude had certainly not reached Luisa and her mother. Lost in thought, Sadie almost missed Angelo's comment, but caught the end of it.

"…festival next week, since you live out of the area."

Realizing he'd either suggested she return for the rescheduled festival or voiced the thought that she couldn't, she replied with the safest comment. "We'll see. I may be able to get away again. I'm sure it will go off without a hitch this time." *Unless the murderer returns to the scene of the crime.*

Luisa entered the tasting room through the back door. Elena was not with her.

"It's nice to see you again," Luisa said to Sadie, though Sadie suspected Luisa's statement was less than sincere. "Thank you for taking the food to the bed and breakfast yesterday. We never could have eaten all that, even with close friends dropping by last night to see how we were doing. I assume it was enjoyed?" Luisa's voice seemed more animated than usual, most likely from the discussion with the mother.

"Yes, it was welcomed eagerly. I had a few nibbles myself." *As did your local law enforcement.* An image of the plastic bagged bruschetta heading out the door ran through Sadie's mind.

Sadie's cell phone rang, and she excused herself to take the call outside. Talking on the phone inside business locations had always struck Sadie as being rude. She particularly disliked the all-too-common occurrence of this in restaurants. She recalled one especially annoying occasion where a single man had two cell phones on his table, both on speakerphone. It was as if he thought he was out to dine with two other people, who chattered away at him while he forked spaghetti into his mouth. Why the restaurant manager never asked the man to put the phones away had always been a mystery to her. Looking back, she regretted not having the nerve at the time to walk over and dump both phones in the man's marinara sauce. She vowed to carry through with this action if the opportunity ever presented itself again, in which case she hoped the offending party would be hovering over an especially creamy bowl of mushroom soup, or perhaps an elaborate bouillabaisse. A sticky stack of syrup-laden pancakes might do, as well.

Sadie walked to an empty corner of the outside patio. Amber's harried voice surprised her. It was rare that anything ruffled the girl's nerves.

"Oh, I'm so glad I was able to reach you! Here…" Sadie heard a thump and wondered if Amber had dropped the phone. She was startled at the sound of Matteo's voice.

"Sadie? You have to help me. I'm in a lot of trouble."

CHAPTER EIGHT

Sadie settled into a corner booth at The Grapevine, a small café located a couple of blocks from Vines and Tines. Perusing the menu, she chose a salad of mixed greens, cranberries, pumpkin seeds and sliced grapes in a lemon-basil vinaigrette. An individual-sized basket of cheddar sourdough bread landed on the table shortly after she placed her order. Turning down an offer for wine – the server had an exceptional suggestion for pairing with the salad – she settled for an iced tea and tried to clear her thoughts.

Matteo's call had been out of the blue, his tone frantic. She'd almost convinced herself that Tina's fishing story was possible, despite the fact it sounded, well, fishy. But the story Matteo told her was, unfortunately, more believable. It was also much more worrisome. Matteo told Sadie he had been communicating with Simon Flanagan during negotiations for the winery sale, which would have transferred ownership to Serrano-Flanagan. The sale would have effectively ended the family business. A venture begun generations ago would have died. The Tremiato family had been in discord over the decision until the majority decided to keep the property and winery in the family.

All that would have been fine, had the deceased accepted the fact the Tremiatos didn't want to sell. Instead, Flanagan had blamed the failure of the proposed business deal on Matteo, who'd decided against selling in the end. Sadie hadn't been able to pry any specific business details out of Matteo. He'd remained tight-lipped, though mentioned there had been hang-up calls recently that he suspected came from inside Serrano-Flanagan. He'd considered those calls harassment, annoying rather than dangerous.

The bigger problem was that Matteo hadn't been fishing. Worse yet, he had set up the loan of the fishing gear with his friend as a ruse to cover being out of town for the night, his intention being to meet the deceased in secret at the winery. That plan hit a rough snag when he arrived at the winery after midnight, expecting to meet a very alive Mr. Flanagan. Except that he wasn't. Alive, that is.

Sadie watched her salad arrive and thought back to her exchange with Matteo on the phone.

"Matteo," Sadie had said, trying to recover from the unexpected shock of the call. "What is going on? People are worried about you. There's been a murder at your family's winery and you're nowhere to be found."

"It wasn't supposed to happen this way." Matteo's voice was so faint Sadie could barely hear him.

"What wasn't supposed to happen this way, Matteo? You're starting to scare me. And why are you whispering?"

A pause. "I'm behind your counter."

"You're hiding behind the store counter?" If she hadn't been so worried, Sadie would have laughed. "Did you tell Amber why you're hiding behind our counter?"

"I just said I was avoiding a pushy customer."

"So tell me what happened."

"I was just supposed to meet him to pass on some information. How was I to know this was a set-up?"

"I'm trying to follow, Matteo. Start over again. Who were you supposed to meet? What information? What set-up?"

"The particular information isn't important," Matteo said, keeping his voice low. "But I'm telling you I was set up. I agreed to meet Simon Flanagan at our family winery, a man I did business with recently."

"Matteo. I don't think I like where this is going." Sadie took a deep breath and urged him on.

"I know, I was foolish," Matteo continued. "Flanagan wanted to stop by the store, but I didn't want him to come here. He suggested meeting in the fermentation building. It would be quiet and out of sight."

"Oh dear, Matteo! What have you done?"

"Nothing! But that's not how it's going to look. They're going to think I killed him."

"Did you?"

"Of course not! He was already dead when I got there. But I didn't wear gloves. Why would I? I thought we were just meeting briefly. I'm sure someone inside the company was setting me up, retaliating because I blocked the sale of our winery. I probably tracked footprints all over the place, too."

"This is not good," Sadie said, thinking back and remembering the crime scene unit dusting the door for fingerprints. No doubt they'd checked for footprints, too.

"What size are your shoes?"

"Thirteen and a half."

"Matteo! This is *really* not good! Why can't your feet be a size nine? Ten, tops?"

"Sadie, it's not my fault if I have big feet!! You are not helping!"

"You're going to need to turn yourself in and explain what happened. Just tell the police the truth. Unless you give them the back story, all they'll have is evidence against you."

"That's just it. I don't have a back story that can be proven. There's no way to explain this. No one from Serrano-Flanagan is going to admit to setting me up."

"What about cell phone records, Matteo?"

"That could be a problem. He's called me repeatedly. Oh, no! I wouldn't be surprised if the calls were bugged! Sadie, you have to get me out of this. I'll owe you chocolate for the rest of my life."

Was he serious?

"That could work," Sadie said, realizing she hadn't had a truffle in more than 48 hours, though the chocolate drizzled cream puffs had helped still the cravings.

"Why do you think the calls were bugged?" Sadie temporarily set aside the thought of free chocolate in favor of more information.

"It...it doesn't matter," Matteo said. His voice dropped to a whisper, as Sadie heard a sales transaction taking place. She could almost see him crouched behind the counter while Amber rang up purchases on the counter above.

The discussion had ended with Sadie offering to dig a little deeper and with Matteo saying he was off to fish, as long as he had the equipment and needed to stay out of sight. He promised not to disappear while Sadie worked on clearing him.

Sadie stabbed a fork into a clump of red leaf lettuce and cranberries, swirling it around the bottom of the plate to soak up some extra lemon-basil dressing. She was enjoying the mix of flavors when a man slid into the chair across from her.

"Sorry to intrude on you, Sadie," Stefano said, reaching for a piece of the cheddar sourdough bread.

"Stefano, nice to see you," Sadie said politely.

"I'm glad I ran into you. I think you might be able to help me."

Maybe the Tremiato family should consider paying her a retainer. Chocolate and wine could be paired, right?

"Does your winery produce a good Port?"

"I beg your pardon?" Stefano paused, his hand suspended in mid-air ready to stuff bread in his mouth.

"Never mind," Sadie said. "How can I help you?"

"It's Tina." Stefano leaned back in the chair like a sultry *GQ* model, catching a few wandering female eyes.

"Oh that poor darling. How is she doing?" Sadie had no idea what to expect from this conversation, but she guessed that Matteo wasn't the only Tremiato pulling her deep into their family affairs.

"I'm so worried about her. Since yesterday's ... events, she's not been herself. You're going to continue staying at The Vintage Vine, right? You know you're safe there." Sadie nodded. "Maybe you can just watch her and make sure she's not too distraught, that she's not saying crazy things that make no sense. Maybe you could let me know if you think I should do something to help, if she seems to be out of control or something, if you sense she might sabotage herself and ... the family."

"It sounds like you want me to spy on your wife." *Oops. Subtlety was never one of her strengths.*

Stefano coughed and sat up straighter. "No, no, of course not! I'm just ... worried."

Sure you are, Sadie thought.

"I don't mind checking on Tina." Stefano coughed again, and Sadie pushed her untouched water glass toward him.

"Maybe Luisa will stop by to see how she's doing?" Sadie suggested. "My sister-in-law was kind enough to check in on me when my last late husband died." This was a fabrication, of course. Morris didn't have a sister as far as Sadie knew, and her other husbands' sisters had been less than fond of Sadie. They found her too brash, too bright, envied her color sense, she was sure. And they always resented the feathers. She hoped Stefano might now reveal something to help crack the enigma that was Luisa Tremiato.

Stefano smiled. "I wouldn't count on that. Those two have never been close."

Sadie took a delicate chance. "I noticed that your mother seems to be quite proud of Tina's bed and breakfast. Does Luisa see your wife as a rival for Mama Elena's approval?" Sadie hoped she wasn't touching a raw nerve.

"Yes. Rivalry or something like it," Stefano said. He frowned, and Sadie knew he wouldn't share anything more about his sister.

"I'm happy to check in with Tina when I get back to the inn. But ... Stefano, couldn't *you* ask her how she's doing?"

Stefano scanned the room, as if distracted. "She confides in other people before me."

Did she note a hint of jealousy?

"Anyone in particular?"

"It's an old story." He gave no further explanation. Instead, he stood up and said, "Thank you for listening, Sadie. I appreciate your kindness to my wife." He walked to the restaurant exit, glanced up and down the sidewalk, and left the café.

"Coco," Sadie said, leaning over the chair next to her and speaking into her tote bag, "this whole family is a little unusual. And their behavior in public is certainly strange." She looked up and smiled at two diners at another table who were staring at her. "Favorite tote bag!"

Sadie finished her salad, paid the check and went back to the inn. She found Tina on the front porch, watering the azalea in the hanging baskets. She hummed a light-hearted tune that Sadie couldn't quite put her finger on, but the word buttercups came to mind. The innkeeper's behavior continued to strike Sadie as odd for a person who had discovered a dead body a mere twenty-four hours before.

"Have you been out sightseeing? We have such a lovely town." Tina climbed down a multi-tiered step stool and moved on to a redwood container of primrose at the top of the porch steps.

"I had lunch at The Grapevine," Sadie said. "Charming little café. I ate a scrumptious salad with cranberries and grapes. Delicious dressing, too!"

"Oh, I love The Grapevine. They make a great roasted tomato-basil soup. I haven't been there for ages, but Stefano…" Her voice trailed off. "Well, we used to meet there for lunch a lot, once guests were checked out and Celia got started on the rooms." Tina gestured toward the inn, undoubtedly indicating that her assistant was there.

"You'll have to try that salad sometime."

Sadie thought about how to proceed with her investigation. She considered the phone call from Matteo to be confidential. If he wanted Tina to know what was going on, he could call her. Or perhaps he had? If not, it would be best to leave Tina with the assumption he'd gone fishing. The fact that he'd indicated to Sadie that he *was* going fishing now lessened the feeling that she was hiding something from Tina.

For now, Sadie decided to stick to small talk until she knew enough to ask the right questions. Back in her room, she settled Coco into her palace before making a quick call to Flair.

"Amber, just checking in. Anything going on?"

"Mrs. Hilbert picked up the scarf she ordered and UPS delivered two cartons."

"Probably those new linen tunics from market. One of my favorite finds at that last trade show. Once we mark them as received, we should display one with those long strands of exotic beads from Peru."

"You do have a sense of style, Sadie."

Sadie laughed. "It's not mere 'style,' my dear. It's called flair. Hence…"

"…the name of the store. Yes, I know."

It was a routine they had, working any fashion discussions around the word, "flair."

"Anyone hiding on the floor behind the counter?"

"Not at the moment," Amber said. "I think he was going fishing."

"Yes, that's what he told me. Any customers of his stopping by?"

"A few. Most just look at the closed sign on his door and leave. Hopefully he'll be back tomorrow. Matteo sure is behaving strangely lately, don't you think? He never closes shop, and I don't think he's ever let a customer intimidate him."

"Maybe he's just tired and needs a break from his work and all those ravenous chocolate lovers, as we all do," Sadie said. "Look at me."

"Yes, and it's about time you took a few days for yourself. Don't worry, everything here will be fine. I'll put the new linen out and redo the front window display to include it."

"Sounds good. Thanks, Amber. Let me know if you hear from Matteo again."

Sadie ended the call and set her cell phone down on a side table. She pulled a book out of her suitcase and headed out to the back garden. Amber was right. She was due for some time for herself. Maybe she'd even find a local day spa and have a facial before heading back to the city the next day.

CHAPTER NINE

The sound of a car door brought Sadie out of a light doze. She'd barely gotten one chapter into her mystery before her eyelids closed and the book settled on her chest. She lifted her head from the chaise lounge and cupped one hand across her forehead like a visor. Except for her car, the guest parking lot beside the inn was empty. But the tip of a black and white vehicle stuck out from the main street.

Sadie closed the book and stood, brushing several leaves off her clothing. Slipping in through the rear entrance, she closed the door softly. Muffled words came from the direction of the kitchen. Entering through the back ensured she wouldn't disturb anyone. And made eavesdropping easier. She tiptoed down the hall until the voices became clear.

"We just have a few more questions to ask you, Mrs. Tremiato. Just to remind you, I'm Detective Hudson and this is Detective Schafer." The man's voice was deep and melodic. Sadie suspected it might have been soothing under different circumstances.

"No problem, detectives. Would you like to sit down? We can talk here in the breakfast area. My only guest is outside, reading."

Sadie pressed against the hallway wall, feeling only slightly guilty for hiding her presence. After all, her intentions were good. She was only trying to help Matteo.

"Thank you," a slightly different voice replied. *Softer? Female?* Sadie fought the urge to peek around the corner. She listened as several chairs scraped the floor, envisioning the trio as they sat. This was good. She'd have enough warning to dash back down the hall if anyone stood up.

"We just want to go over a few statements you made at the station yesterday." Sadie heard the sound of papers being shuffled.

"I told you everything I know," Tina said. The innkeeper's voice seemed calm, yet guarded.

"I'm sure you did." The voice matched Detective Hudson, the officer who had spoken first. Sadie pegged him as the primary.

"You told us you found the victim's body on the floor, is that correct?"

"Yes," Tina said.

More papers shuffled. "Is there a chance you tried to move the body at all?"

"What?" Tina's response sounded like a cross between a laugh and a snort. "Are you kidding me? Do I look like I could move a body twice my size?"

"Honestly, ma'am, no. But we think someone tried to move him. There were smudge marks on his arms."

"Well, if so, someone else must have done that. I told you already he was right where I found him. Already dead, as I've pointed out many times." Tina's voice quavered.

"I know this must be hard for you," Detective Schafer said. "But think back to when you found the body and then went to the farmhouse to call the police. When the officers on duty yesterday arrived, you took them back into the..." Her voice trailed off.

"Fermentation building," Tina filled in. "Yes. They asked me to. I didn't want to go back in there, not with..."

"Of course not," Detective Schafer said. "That's understandable."

"But they probably wanted to see my reaction, thinking I might be guilty."

Detective Hudson cleared his throat.

"That's not really how it works," Detective Schafer added quickly. "It was just important to document exactly what you saw, to hear it from you while it was fresh in your mind."

"Something else." *Detective Hudson again.*

A light tap followed the statement, as if someone had dropped something small on the table.

"Have you seen this before?"

A pause, then Tina's voice. "No, I haven't. What is it?"

"That's what we're trying to find out. We think it's a lapel pin, the kind you might get as a travel souvenir."

Or at a culinary trade show. Sadie closed her eyes and shook her head. *Oh, Matteo!* she thought.

"What does that have to do with anything?" Tina clearly sounded frustrated now.

"It was found in the...fermentation building, about ten feet from Mr. Flanagan's body."

"Well, I don't remember seeing it. I would have told you if I had."

"I'm not saying you saw it, ma'am. I just thought you might recognize it."

"I'm sorry, I can't help you."

Interesting choice of words, Sadie noted. Tina might have said she didn't recognize it, but not saying so implied that she did. Then again, maybe not. The relationship between Tina and Matteo was still hazy to Sadie. On one hand, it was possible they were simply a brother and sister-in-law who got along well with each other. Or Tina could be covering for him for some reason, which would explain her drastic change in behavior after the day of the murder – or murder discovery, if that happened to be the case, since the police hadn't disclosed the time of death. The connection between Tina and Matteo could be deeper and more complicated than it appeared. Since Matteo never mentioned Tina, Sadie found this last thought hard to believe. But she couldn't rule out anything. She needed to keep her mind open when she put on her crime-solving hat.

The sound of a chair scooting cautioned Sadie to scurry down the hallway, which meant the voices would be out of earshot. Frustrated, she entered her room but kept the door ajar enough to follow any major movements. She soon heard more chairs against the floor, then an exchange of polite farewells that she couldn't quite make out and the sound of the front door closing.

Sadie decided that she absolutely must have a cup of coffee or tea, but she waited several minutes before sauntering out to the front of the inn so that Tina wouldn't guess that Sadie had known the police were there. Then she went in search of both beverage and information.

Prepared to ask Tina for coffee, she arrived upfront to hear a faint conversation and to view the innkeeper through the kitchen door. Pacing back and forth, Tina whispered into a cell phone. Sadie couldn't be certain, but suspected it was Matteo. Had Tina rushed to fill him in on the visit from the police? To warn him? Or was she talking to Matteo at all? Perhaps she'd called Stefano. Sadie strained to hear a name, but couldn't catch anything but murmurs. When the phone call ended, she feigned interest in an empty coffee pot on the buffet table while waiting for Tina to emerge.

"I see you've come in from the garden," Tina said. "I didn't want to disturb you once you'd fallen asleep. A spontaneous nap is one of the luxuries of a mini-vacation."

Sadie tossed out her best innocent laugh. "Oh, yes, reading often makes me sleepy. I had no chance because of the warm sun and that peaceful atmosphere. I thought a cup of coffee might bring me around. Or tea."

"I'll make a pot of coffee," Tina said, starting for the kitchen.

"Oh, I don't want to trouble you," Sadie said. "I was just going to grab something if it happened to be on the buffet."

"It's no trouble, in fact I could use a cup myself," Tina called over her shoulder. "I usually do have it on the buffet in case guests want it midday." Her voice grew distant as she continued to speak from the kitchen. Sadie heard the sound of running water and the whir of a coffee grinder. The words faded in and out as the coffee-making sounds continued.

"...lost track of time...as if I would know..." Sadie strained to hear, but couldn't catch it all.

"You should have heard them," Tina said as she finally came through the kitchen door. "It was like I was being accused of not admitting something I didn't even know." She poured two cups of coffee and set the coffee pot on a warming unit, flipping the switch to an "on" position. "What do you think, Sadie? I feel like they don't believe anything I say."

Sadie took the coffee from Tina and took a sip, buying time to think of the best response. Did *she* even believe Tina? She had no reason not to, yet there were too many pieces that didn't fall together. Why had Tina been at the winery that morning? What about her hushed phone call? What about her odd response to the detectives' question about the pin? If only she could ask about it, but that would give away the fact that she'd been listening. Perhaps she could draw it out of her. She reminded herself that Tina didn't know she'd overheard the detectives' visit.

"Tina, do you mean the police? Were they here?" The two women sat down at the table. She took another sip of coffee and watched Tina. The conflicted look on the innkeeper's face told Sadie Tina wasn't sure how much to divulge. To Sadie's relief, she chose to confide in her.

"Yes, the two detectives stopped by a little while ago. I guess you didn't hear me from the kitchen. Sorry about that. I was talking to Matteo on the phone. I do tend to talk without paying attention to whether people are listening or not."

"I couldn't quite hear you over the coffee grinder," Sadie said quickly. "I wasn't listening carefully." *Pants on fire.*

Tina set her coffee cup on the table. "There were a couple things they brought up. Apparently someone tried to move the...Mr. Flanagan."

"Really? How would they know that?"

"Some sort of smudges on his arms. Does that even make sense?"

"Well, I suppose if someone grasped his arms, that might have left marks."

"Maybe. I don't know." Tina sighed. "I've never watched any of those police shows on TV."

"What else did they have to say?"

"They found some sort of pin and wondered if I remembered seeing it."

"Did you?"

"I don't think so. It did look familiar, but I couldn't place it. Maybe just a souvenir pin from another winery? But I didn't recognize the logo and I know almost all the wineries in the area."

"I'd love to see it," Sadie said. "Any chance they left it?" She already knew the answer.

Tina shook her head. "They said it was evidence and they had to keep it. But they gave me a picture of it." She slid a color snapshot over to Sadie. The pin looked to be about one half inch by three quarters of an inch. A gold cursive "C" filled a good portion of it. The background was a cobalt blue.

Sadie handed the photo back to Tina, who put it away. She was sure she'd seen the pin's logo before, but couldn't place it. She'd stick with the idea of a culinary show. Matteo usually went to those and always came back with a canvas bag filled with purchase orders and samples. Sadie often hovered nearby when he returned from those events, hoping to catch a taste of some new delectable treat. Maybe he'd picked up a pin at one of the booths.

The sound of the front door opening and closing broke into the **conversation**, and Stefano entered the room. He said hello to Tina and displayed one of his attractive smiles upon seeing Sadie. Returning the smile, Sadie knew he most likely interpreted the sight of the two women together as a follow-up to his earlier request at the café.

Stefano poured himself a cup of coffee from the buffet and set it on the table.

"Any sugar?"

"In the cupboard, same place as always," Tina said.

Stefano grabbed the sugar and took a seat, dropping a casual kiss on Tina's cheek as he rounded the table.

"What are you doing here in the middle of your workday, Stefano?"

"A customer said he saw a police car parked out front a short while ago. I just came over to see if everything was OK." He placed a hand on top of Tina's, but Tina pulled it away and tucked a lock of hair behind her ear.

"Oh, that," Tina said. "Yes, a couple of detectives stopped by to go over some things from yesterday. Just routine."

"No new developments?"

Sadie wondered why she felt as if something was hidden under the surface of Stefano's comments and questions. Maybe it was that he always seemed to be playing a part. Plus he seemed pretty darned cheerful compared to his mood earlier in the day. Was this a show for Tina, to keep her from worrying? Was he truly concerned for her, or just using this meeting to do some snooping of his own?

"Nothing new," Tina said. Sadie noted she chose not to share the information about the pin and wondered why not.

Sadie looked back and forth between the two as if they were opponents in a tennis match. Except this particular game felt more dangerous. She also couldn't help but wonder how much of Stefano's concerned, affectionate manner was because of her presence. She decided to put that theory to a test.

"Excuse me. I'm in need of the powder room."

Sadie slipped out of the dining area, leaving her coffee cup behind to imply she'd be right back. She walked down the hall, opened and closed the door to her room, but stayed in the hallway, where she could still hear.

"Is there something you're not telling me, Tina?" Stefano said.

"There's nothing new." Tina's voice was weary. "Just don't worry."

"Of course I'll worry." Stefano's tone grew more insistent. "I care about you, Tina. I wish you'd believe that."

"You care about your business, your family, yourself and your adoring fans at the store."

"Don't start in on that again, Tina. I do everything I can to reassure you that you're important to me." A pause. A clink of a coffee cup against the wooden surface of the table. "Now tell me, did the police come up with any new clues? Maybe some new evidence?"

"Why would you even ask that, Stefano?"

Indeed, why?

"I figured they had something new to say or they wouldn't have stopped by."

"They just wanted to double check some statements I made yesterday."

Sadie opened and closed the door to her room again and returned to the front. Stefano displayed his usual, charming smile when Sadie walked in. It was an expression she was beginning to distrust.

She wasn't sure she trusted anyone in the Tremiato family at this point.

CHAPTER TEN

Luisa was behind the counter of the tasting room when Sadie walked in. Late afternoon sun flowed through the windows bouncing off wine glasses that hung from a suspended rack. A feeling in the air said the day was almost over. And, with only twenty minutes before the tasting room closed, it almost was.

"Still in town, I see," Luisa said. She glanced at Sadie briefly before looking back down. "We're closing up soon." *Nice to see you, too.*

"I won't take long," Sadie said, putting forth a double dose of cheer. "I'm heading home in the morning and just wanted to pick up a couple of bottles of your excellent Chardonnay. And to see how your mother is doing." She knew that sounded nosy, but a tidbit of information about the animated discussion she witnessed between mother and daughter before could be helpful.

Luisa nodded, even made eye contact again. "She's still upset about recent events, but will be fine." She changed the subject immediately. "I can help you with the wine." Turning away, she took two bottles from a multi-tiered wine holder and placed them on the counter. "Two?"

"Yes, two will do. And…I saw some things in your gift section…" Sadie moved to the corner display that she'd studied when she first arrived. She picked out four dangling wine glass charms, each with different grape designs so that drinks could be identified individually. She'd seen those used at parties on occasion and had always wanted a set. She added a pair of earrings with clusters of grapes to match the charms. It was an unusual combination of items, but unique for a future cocktail occasion.

"Ah, beautiful choices," Luisa said as Sadie returned with the items in hand. "Those are both handmade by a local artist." Wrapping them in tissue, Luisa slid them into a paper bag with the Tremiato logo on it. She rang up the purchases and waited while Sadie rummaged through her tote bag for her wallet. A tiny yip resulted, which Luisa either didn't hear or simply ignored.

"Yes, whimsical," Sadie said as she handed a credit card across the counter. "I hope your mother is doing better, by the way."

Luisa dismissed the statement with a simple "thank you." She handed the credit card transaction slip back to be signed and packaged the wine bottles to prevent breakage. "I hope you'll come back to see us again sometime," she said as she turned over the purchases. Sadie wasn't sure she'd ever heard a less sincere invitation,

"Oh, she will." Angelo stepped behind the counter and stood next to Luisa, who didn't budge one millimeter. "You'll come back next weekend for the rescheduled festival, right?" He turned to Luisa with a bright smile. "We're hoping everyone will come back, aren't we, Luisa?" Getting no response, he turned to Sadie. "We may even get others who wouldn't have been here this weekend. It all works out, one way or another. After all, there's no such thing as bad publicity, right?"

"I'll do my best," Sadie answered. Using murder as a marketing tactic seemed, well, tacky.

"I don't think you ever said what you do." Luisa's sudden question caught Sadie off guard. It seemed odd that she'd ask her that just as she was leaving.

"I have a business in the city." Both Angelo and Luisa stared at her, expectantly, as if she'd trailed off after a sentence fragment.

"I have a little boutique that sells unique clothes and accessories, nothing major. Not nearly as exciting as running a family winery." Sadie was eager to leave now before a connection could be made between her shop and Matteo's.

"I'll carry those for you," Angelo said. He moved quickly after watching Sadie try to pick up both wine bottles, and the bag of glass trinkets, while holding her tote bag cautiously beside her. He accompanied Sadie to her car and reached into the back seat, placing the wine bottles on their side.

"Thank you, Angelo. I'll do my best to come back." Sadie set her tote bag down on the passenger seat and gave him what she hoped was a casual smile. With wine, trinkets and tote bag safely loaded, she said goodbye and headed back to The Vintage Vine for one last night before returning to the city.

* * *

At the inn, Sadie found an unfamiliar blue Lincoln Continental in the parking lot. She was certain Tina had said there weren't any new guests arriving that night, and the few remaining from the weekend were the quiet sort. She was curious.

Sadie parked her car a few spots down from the Continental. She placed the bottles of wine in her trunk, along with the other purchases, and glanced up at the sky, where a few light gray clouds were gathering. She put the top up, in case the clouds turned ominous, and then bustled in through the back door. It only took a few minutes to get Coco settled in her palace and fill her China bowls with food and fresh water. She then went in search of a glass of whatever Tremiato specialty the inn had out on the buffet.

"Oh, Sadie, I'm glad to see you!" An enthusiastic Tina was just placing a tray of Brie, crackers and sliced pears out next to a bottle of Petite Sirah. "We have another guest tonight – a walk-in – so I spruced up the wine hour a bit. I'm bringing out a plate of those stuffed mushrooms, too. And I'll put some coffee out later, along with the rest of those cream puffs. Maybe we can finish everything off. I hate to see food go to waste, don't you?" Without waiting for an answer, Tina disappeared into the kitchen.

Sadie's eyes lit up. The idea of having an entire dinner of chocolate drizzled cream puffs was appealing, especially if she could justify it as doing her part in community service. She was certainly in favor of not wasting food. However, she reigned in her sweet tooth and poured herself a glass of sirah. The contrast to the chardonnay that she'd had several times over the weekend was satisfying. She was glad she'd added another night to her stay. She spread some Brie on a cracker, topped it off with a sliver of pear, and sashayed to the front parlor, following a trail of soft jazz. This is where she found the unexpected guest, an elderly man easily in his 80s, though it was difficult to gauge for certain, since he rested on the couch, a golf cap pulled so low over his face it nearly touched his bushy salt and pepper mustache. A cane rested on the floor beside him.

"Here, Mr. Collins..." Tina's voice trailed off as she rounded the parlor corner and saw Sadie's finger pressed to her lips. "Oh, I'm not surprised he's asleep," she whispered. "He looked exhausted when he first arrived. That was a couple of hours ago. Said he'd meant to drive right through this area, but was feeling tired and thought it best not to push." Tina backed out of the room so the guest could rest, Sadie right behind her.

"Always smart to get off the road in that case," Sadie agreed. She gulped more wine and took another bite of the Brie-cracker-pear combo, crumbs tumbling to the floor.

"He's staying in the room next to yours. Normally, when we only have a few guests, I try to spread the rooms out. But you saw the cane...I couldn't put him upstairs."

Sadie waved her hand in the air shooing away Tina's worries. "It's fine," she said. *He'll probably sleep the whole evening, anyway.* "Any word from Matteo?"

Tina shook her head. "I bet he gives me a call tomorrow. I'm sure he's still out fishing now, or on his way back." She disappeared into the kitchen, returning with a tray of stuffed mushrooms, which she added to the buffet.

"You're not worried?" Sadie still wasn't buying Tina's offhand attitude about Matteo's whereabouts.

"No. And I don't think you should be, either. I'm sure he'll be back at his shop tomorrow when you get home."

Sadie popped a stuffed mushroom in her mouth, sat at the table, and set her wine glass down. "Well, I hope so," she said. "I'm in dire need of one of his raspberry truffles."

"Aren't those the best?" Tina laughed. Sadie decided to use the light moment to dig a little more.

"Tina, about that article in the paper this morning covering yesterday's events. I know you said Stefano and Angelo dealt with winery business, but are you sure you don't remember anything about the failed merger or sale? Could this have had something to do with Mr. Flanagan's murder?"

"Oh, those 'negotiations'! It was all such a mess I tried to block it out. All I know is that the family turned down the offer, but that whole process was like a Shakespearean tragedy when it came to taking sides."

"What do you mean?" Sadie had found an opening.

Tina poured herself a glass of wine and sat next to Sadie. "I'll tell you, I've never seen the Tremiato family at such odds with each other before. That Serrano-Flanagan offer was a decent one – plenty of money. Stefano thought it was a good deal, enough to keep Elena secure for the rest of her life, plus plenty to go around to the rest of the family. Angelo agreed with Stefano. But Elena wouldn't hear of it. She said the winery was a family legacy and should stay in the family. Said it would tarnish the Tremiato name if another company took over."

"And Luisa?"

"Luisa? Luisa always wants whatever Luisa wants. In this case, it was probably the money. But she won't ever go against Elena, so her 'public' position was to not sell."

Sadie took another sip of wine. "So it sounds like the family was split male versus female on this issue."

"Not entirely. Matteo was against selling, though he debated in favor at first."

"Was he involved with the discussions? I thought he was estranged from the family."

"Not legally," Tina explained. "He's still family as far as the law is concerned. And he has the majority interest. They had to ask his opinion."

"Who talked to him about it?"

"Angelo. Though I understand it was a brief conversation, and not a pleasant one."

"Why?"

"There's always been friction since Matteo left to open his business, especially with Angelo. This just made it worse."

"Why especially with Angelo?"

"Because he was left with the winery to run. He felt it shouldn't have become his sole responsibility, that Matteo should have stayed around to help."

"But he has Luisa to help. And why doesn't Angelo resent Stefano having his own business, if he resents Matteo's business that much?"

"Angelo is very old school. His father was the same way. The Tremiato men don't think women have a place in business. And Vines and Tines was actually Elena's idea, not Stefano's. The store feeds people into the winery, not to mention selling the product itself."

"So Angelo perceives Matteo as abandoning the family, whereas Stefano is helping by sending more business their way," Sadie mused.

"Exactly," Tina said.

"It sounds like Elena is a smart businesswoman," Sadie said. The irony that Elena, a woman, was the power behind the business didn't escape Sadie.

"Very," Tina agreed. "Whatever goes on in that family comes down to Elena. Gustavo always handled the business side of the winery, but Elena stepped up as soon as he passed away. She's stronger than the rest of them combined. They'll all argue, but in the end they won't go against her wishes."

"Except Matteo," Sadie pointed out.

"Yes, except Matteo. That's another reason the family resents him going out on his own. They feel he let his mother down. He's always been independent, able to stand on his own. He's not afraid of anything."

Sadie fought the urge to smile, as she pictured Matteo hiding on the floor behind the counter at Flair.

CHAPTER ELEVEN

The click of a door closing roused Sadie from sleep. Wine, conversation and enough appetizers to constitute a hearty dinner had lulled her into an early bedtime. Her attempts to stay up reading had been futile, so she'd set her book aside and turned out the light before ten o'clock.

Now awake, she realized the sound she'd heard was the shutting of the door to Mr. Collins' room. He'd retired even earlier than she had, leaving the front parlor without a word to anyone. Had it not been for the slow, dull tapping of his cane against the wood hallway floor, she and Tina wouldn't have known he'd moved.

Sadie glanced at the clock next to her bed: two o'clock in the morning. An odd time to be up and about, she thought. Mr. Collins' room, like hers, had a private bath. So he wasn't in need of a middle of the night restroom jaunt, as some upper floor rooms that shared a bath down the hall might require. Had he gone in search of a glass of water? Leftover appetizers perhaps? Or maybe he was a sleepwalker. Sadie amused herself with the possibilities.

Finally letting curiosity win, she tiptoed to her door and cracked it open, glancing down the hallway, where she saw an oddly spry Mr. Collins slip out the front door, overnight bag and cane in hand. She pursed her lips. The old man had barely been able to tap his way down the hall earlier. Why the sudden burst of agility?

Sadie slipped out of her room and reached the front of the inn just in time to hear a car start up outside. She glanced out the window, surprised to see the blue Lincoln Continental backing out of the lot. When she moved to the registration desk, she saw a lone key sitting on the counter. She glanced into Mr. Collins' room as she returned to hers to find it empty of personal belongings. He had simply left in the middle of the night.

"I don't understand this, Coco," she said, once settled back into her bed. "The person I saw slip out the front door moved too quickly to be Mr. Collins, yet I'm sure it was." Coco yipped in agreement. "There's only one conclusion I can draw from this," Sadie continued. "Mr. Collins was not Mr. Collins."

Again Coco yipped. Sadie smiled as she slid back under the quilt. It was nice to have a traveling companion who agreed with everything she said.

* * *

The breakfast room was busy when Sadie emerged the next morning. Several guests sat together, planning visits to various tasting rooms in the area. Tina spoke with a guest who was checking out. Sadie poured a cup of coffee from the buffet and placed a bear claw on a plate, adding several slices of melon to balance the good calories against the bad.

"We're emptying out today, all but a few rooms," Tina said, finally getting a chance to say good morning to Sadie. "Several guests have already taken coffee to go and checked out. And one must have left early this morning, because his key was on the counter when I woke up."

"That would be Mr. Collins, I imagine," Sadie said.

"Yes," Tina said. "How did you know?"

"Actually, I saw him leave. I heard a door close in the middle of the night and looked out into the hall, just in time to see him go out the front door."

"How odd," Tina said. "He just checked in yesterday. Strange elderly man."

"I'm not convinced of the elderly part."

"What do you mean?" Tina looked confused.

"I watched the way he moved as he left – quickly, easily. He didn't use his cane; he carried it." Sadie paused. "How did he pay? Did he give you a credit card?"

"No, as a matter of fact," Tina said. "He paid cash. Said he preferred that when he travels. Some sort of safety paranoia about using credit cards."

"Yes," Sadie agreed. "Some sort of paranoia is right. But I don't think it's about using credit cards. I think he didn't want to leave a real name."

"You're saying he wasn't who he said he was? That he was pretending to be Mr. Collins?"

Sadie nodded. "More than that, Tina. I doubt there even is a Mr. Collins."

"You're saying he was here in disguise?"

"Yes," Sadie said. "A younger man disguised as an old man, under a false name."

"But why?"

"I don't know," Sadie said. "But I'm guessing it has something to do with Mr. Flanagan's murder. Maybe even connecting you to the murder. Why else would this guest pretending to be someone else choose to stay here just when events unraveled at the winery?" Sadie paused before continuing. "I don't think it's a coincidence."

"Hold that thought." Tina left Sadie to enjoy her coffee and pastry while she made the rounds, refilling guest's coffee cups and thanking a smiling young couple who turned in their room key.

"Honeymooners, those two." Tina said as she returned to Sadie's table. "So sweet. I remember those days. Seems like a long time ago, though. Now...well, you know how it is with Stefano. Seems we always believe it will last forever when we start out."

"I think Stefano still cares for you, Tina," Sadie said. "More than you think. He seemed sincerely worried about you when I ran into him at The Grapevine the other day."

"Don't be fooled. He's a very good actor; he's skilled at creating false impressions. You haven't met the person I know when no one else is around. He can't be trusted."

Before Sadie could push for more information about Stefano's theatrical abilities, Tina needed to return to the registration desk to help another guest check out. Sadie wondered if she'd fallen for Stefano's acting ability when he'd pleaded for Sadie to help Tina. He'd seemed sincere, but could what seemed like sincerity have been a cover for something else?

The inner workings of the Tremiato family were complex and confusing. From what Sadie had observed, any one of them might be capable of murder. At least capable of having a motive. The question was which one? And why?

CHAPTER TWELVE

The trip back to San Francisco was uneventful, other than the annoying traffic that accompanied a Monday morning southbound trip on the 101. A Sunday return would have been easier, but the extra night at The Vintage Vine had been worth it. Not only had it given Sadie a chance to visit with the family members again, but she had been there to witness the unusual behavior of the supposed Mr. Collins. There wasn't a chance in the world that he was the elderly guest he posed as. But why the disguise? And what was he looking to accomplish that involved the inn, or more likely, Tina?

Amber was behind the counter when Sadie arrived at Flair. A shallow brown shipping carton sat open, bright fabric flowing over one edge.

"Ah, I see the silk scarves arrived," Sadie said. She paused to lift one out of the box, admiring a dazzling abstract pattern in purple and red. "Perfect for the Red Hat Society customers."

"Exactly what I thought," Amber said. "But not the most important detail this morning. For one thing, we've had several hang-up calls already, which is freaking me out. For another, as much as I'm eager for you to fill me in, Matteo is waiting for you in your back office."

"Oh, that's a relief," Sadie said. "I thought I'd have to track him down."

"Besides, you need chocolate," Amber added.

"Yes, that, too."

"And if you can calm him down, maybe he'll open his shop." Amber leaned forward slightly to emphasize the importance of this point.

"You're right," Sadie agreed, imagining standing in front of an assortment of treats, possibly that very afternoon. "I'll talk to him."

Of course, it wasn't just about the chocolate, as much fun as it was to joke about. Matteo was either in serious trouble, or needed to prove he wasn't. Even after all the years she'd known him, she had to stay objective. *Everyone is a potential suspect,* she reminded herself. *Don't rule anyone out."* And if the most he was planning to do was hide behind Flair's counter or in Sadie's office, she had her work cut out for her.

Sadie found Matteo sitting in an armchair that she kept in the corner of her office. It was a favorite piece of furniture, as comfortable as it was ugly. Though she did most of her work at a sturdy, Mission style desk, there were times when a sleuth just needed a place to take a cat nap. The chair filled that purpose.

As soon as Sadie walked in, Matteo stood up and began to talk and pace before she had a chance to sit down. This didn't surprise her. She had plenty of questions to ask him, but took advantage of his frantic energy to hear a stream-of-consciousness version of what he had to say. She placed her tote bag on the floor, reached in and lifted Coco out. Obediently, the Yorkie ran to the front of the store, where Amber would get her settled into her usual spot, a velvet cushion on the sales counter.

"This is crazy," Matteo burst out as Sadie sat behind her desk. "I only went to the winery to meet the guy. How was I to know I'd walk in to find him dead? You know I'm going to be accused of this. My fingerprints will be on the doorknob and my footprints are probably all over the place. I was set up, don't you see? Someone else wanted him dead and set up the meeting to make it look like I did it."

"Maybe," Sadie said.

"Maybe?" Matteo repeated. "How can you say maybe? I think it's obvious!"

Sadie shook her head, the new clusters of glass grapes swinging from her ears as she did. "Nothing is obvious in a murder case, Matteo. If something looks obvious, it's too simple. Maybe Mr. Flanagan wasn't even the intended victim. He could have just been there at the wrong time."

"Well, obviously he was there at the wrong time," Matteo said. "But if he wasn't the intended victim, then who…oh, no! Don't even go there!"

"I'm just saying it's necessary to look at every possibility."

"Well, count me out as a possibility, please!" Matteo's face blanched. "I didn't have any enemies."

"You don't know that for sure," Sadie pointed out. "For one thing, there's a lot of animosity toward you in your family."

"No, that's absurd," Matteo shouted, causing Amber to poke her head inside the office and whisper, "Customers!"

"For what it's worth, Matteo, I agree with you," Sadie said. "Disapproving of your career choice is a far cry from wanting you dead. Whoever did this was after someone else, whether Mr. Flanagan or not. And speaking of your career choice…" Sadie was interrupted by an incoming call on her desk phone.

"Hello." She held a finger in front of her lips to signal Matteo to be quiet. "Yes, I made it back just fine." She paused and listened. "I'm surprised they did that." Another pause followed, during which Sadie raised her eyebrows and looked at Matteo. "Indeed, how strange." She watched Matteo, who frowned with frustration, unable to hear the other side of the conversation. After several more sentences, she excused herself, saying she was needed in the front of the store, but would be in touch. Little white lies only weighed lightly on her conscience.

"Well?" Matteo ran both hands through his black hair, making him look more desperate than ever.

Sadie leaned forward and tapped an orange highlighter against the surface of her desk. "That was Tina."

"What? Why didn't you let me talk to her?"

"Because I didn't want her to know you were here, Matteo," Sadie said. "But that's neither here nor there. What's important is that there's new information. The police picked Tina up again this morning for more questioning. The fingerprint analysis came back and showed hers were on the doorknob, which was to be expected.

"And?"

"And nothing."

"Nothing? What do you mean nothing? You're saying my fingerprints didn't show up?"

"That's exactly what I'm saying. Tina's were the only ones they found."

"That doesn't make sense," Matteo said, clearly torn between relief and confusion. "Mine should have been on there, too."

"Yes, I would think so," Sadie agreed. "In fact, there should have been others on there, as well. People go in and out of that building all the time, it seems."

"That's true," Matteo agreed. "But what about Tina? Are they holding her?"

Sadie shook her head. "No, they let her go. The medical examiner's report shows the time of death around ten o'clock the night before. The bed and breakfast was full that night. She has at least a dozen potential witnesses who could confirm she was at the inn at that time. I happen to be one of them. She was baking muffins for the following morning. She didn't go out."

"I'm glad she's in the clear. But that still doesn't explain why my fingerprints didn't show up."

"I can only think of one reason," Sadie said. "Someone must have wiped the door handle clean sometime after you left and before Tina arrived in the morning."

"Who? And why?" Matteo stopped pacing and sat down.

Sadie shook her head. "I don't know the answer to either of those questions. But when we find out, I think we'll have our killer."

CHAPTER THIRTEEN

Sadie leaned back in her favorite overstuffed chair, plopping one furry red slipper up on the matching ottoman, then the other. Silver metallic pompoms bobbed back and forth on each slipper, causing the footwear to pick up a shimmer from the overhead track lighting. She pulled the lower folds of her matching chenille robe over her knees and picked up a goblet of wine from a side table. She'd specifically detoured from Tremiato wine, instead pulling a bottle of French Burgundy from a small collection in her dining room. A little distance from the animated Italian family might do her some good, or at least allow her some objectivity.

Looking out over the scenic San Francisco skyline, Sadie took advantage of the quiet to run recent events through her mind. On the one hand, each Tremiato family member she'd met seemed crazy enough to be involved with a murder, though Matteo and Tina both struck her as slightly more sane than the rest. On the other hand, not one person seemed to have a motive for killing a man connected to a business that had dropped its involvement with the winery. Except...well, she hated to even think of it...but someone being pressured might be motivated to get rid of the pressure. Was Matteo capable of that? She doubted it. He seemed far too stressed to have pulled off something like that.

Stefano, however, aside from his concern over Tina, seemed far calmer. How genuine was that concern? That was a tough question.

Sadie set the wine down and watched Coco tear across the floor with a stuffed velvet lobster in her mouth, a souvenir from a case she'd solved in New England. The red fabric toy matched her bathrobe almost perfectly.

Luisa was too hard to read. Clearly loyal to her mother, she obviously resented the inferior position her brothers put her in as far as business matters were concerned. But there wasn't any direct connection between Luisa and Mr. Flanagan or the Serrano-Flanagan acquisition deal that Sadie could see. Angelo and Matteo seemed to have handled most of that. The friction between Luisa and her brothers seemed like normal sibling rivalry, though with a sexist slant. The male members of the family felt they were better equipped to run the winery.

Tina didn't seem to be subjected to the same condescending viewpoint, but she was running an entirely different type of business, one that the men folk probably thought appropriate for a woman. Plus, she wasn't a Tremiato by birth, only by marriage. That had to play a part, too.

Who else was there? Elena? Sadie thought back to the family matriarch's statement the morning the body was discovered. *"I told him he'd be sorry if he didn't stay away."* No, in spite of that comment, Elena had been far too upset that morning. Either she was an Oscar-caliber actress, or she had nothing to do with the murder. And Angelo just didn't seem like a strong enough personality to have anything to do with the whole mess. But Sadie didn't know him any better than she knew Luisa. Perhaps he had hidden depths of rage.

Dean Martin's voice interrupted Sadie's thoughts, startling her. She'd forgotten she'd changed her ring tone to "That's Amore" upon her return to San Francisco. She set the wine goblet down as gently as possible and grabbed her phone, to see Tina's now-recognizable phone number.

"Sadie," Tina blurted out before Sadie could even say hello. "The police have picked me up again! I'm being set up, I'm sure of it now."

"What are you talking about?" Sadie watched the red lobster disappear under the sofa. This didn't surprise her at all. Coco had never been fond of Dean Martin.

"They showed up this evening with a warrant, asking to search the inn a *third* time. How ridiculous is that? Said they'd gotten an anonymous tip and had to follow through."

Probably looking for more bruschetta, Sadie thought.

"But why did they pick you up? Sadie asked. "They couldn't have found anything they didn't find the first two times."

"But they *did!*" Tina cried. "And that's what doesn't make sense. You know they searched thoroughly before and didn't find anything. But now, suddenly, they found a cork in the kitchen cabinet." Tina's voice fell away as she sobbed. A full minute passed before she regained her composure. "You see why I'm saying I'm being set up? They would have found that before if it had been there. Someone planted it. That's the only thing that could have happened."

"Well…" Sadie paused, uncertain what to say next. Tina was understandably distraught, but Sadie's best approach would be to stay impartial — or at least rational. Someone needed to be, and it certainly wasn't going to be Tina, not at this point. Sadie searched for a soothing response, but Tina spoke before Sadie could come up with anything.

"I'm sure it was Stefano," Tina said, still choking back sobs. "I told you he can't be trusted. And you know he was there after the second time they searched the inn. You sat at the table with us. You saw him go to the cupboard to get sugar — that *same* cupboard where they found the cork. Don't you see, Sadie? He planted it there, all the while coming by during the workday to supposedly see how I was doing. Why won't people believe me?" Again, Tina dissolved into sobs, and Sadie heard an official-sounding voice telling her it was time to hang up. With a muddled goodbye, the line went dead.

Sadie pressed a few buttons, put the phone down and picked up her wine as Coco peeked out from under the couch. "It's safe to come out, Coco," she said. "I've changed the ringtone to Santana, just for you."

Tina had a point. Stefano had arrived quite unexpectedly just after the detectives left the second time. And he *had* gone to the cupboard for sugar. He could have easily slid the cork in there as he removed the sugar. It was convenient timing, for sure. But it was also too obvious. Stefano didn't seem like someone who'd set up a trap that could lead back to him so easily. If the cork was planted, it had to be by someone more obscure. *For example, the kind of someone who walks into an inn using a cane and walks out without needing it.*

CHAPTER FOURTEEN

Sadie arrived at Flair the next morning to find Amber enjoying a dark chocolate truffle, one of a dozen or so that filled a small tray on the store's front counter.

"Matteo opened his shop today, I take it." Sadie leaned forward, looking over the selection. She chose one that promised coconut inside and popped it unto her mouth.

Amber wrapped her hands around a coffee mug and took a sip, eyeing Sadie carefully.

"You don't look as excited as I thought you'd be, Sadie. You were practically in withdrawal when you returned from your weekend." Pushing the chocolate aside, she took Sadie's tote bag from her and lifted Coco out, setting her down in her usual spot.

"I have mixed feelings," Sadie admitted. Amber raised an eyebrow. Sadie was never ambivalent toward chocolate. "Not about the chocolate, of course. And I'm glad to see the shop open," she continued. "I'm sure Matteo lost business the last few days. But I'm not sure opening was a wise decision."

"You think he's in danger?"

"I'm not sure," Sadie admitted. "But I think it's possible. I wish he had an assistant who could run the shop while this whole thing gets resolved."

"He's never wanted anyone to help him," Amber said. "I've had *so* many friends who wanted to work there, but he never hires anyone."

"Matteo likes to be in control. And this is his life, running that business," Sadie added. "He doesn't mind working every day."

"Except the last couple of days," Amber pointed out. "I've never seen him freaked out like that. I guess it makes sense. It's not every day you find out someone was murdered on your family's property."

"No, it's not every day," Sadie repeated, not wanting to share the additional details surrounding Matteo's involvement. It was complicated enough without Amber tossing in her animated two cents' worth. Sadie often wanted to include her in the specifics of her cases, but chose to keep a line between shop business and investigative affairs.

A bell chimed as a customer entered. The older woman headed immediately to a sale area at the back of the shop, and began flipping through a display of discounted sweaters. She lifted a purple cardigan off the rack and held it up in front of herself, before a mirror.

"I see Mrs. Abernathy is still looking at the same sweater." Sadie lowered her voice enough that only Amber could hear.

"Every day," Amber whispered.

"Ten bucks says she buys it by the end of the week." Sadie grinned, waiting for Amber to take the bait.

"You're on!"

Sadie disappeared into the back office to set down her empty tote bag and purse. She checked her voice mail, finding only two messages, one about a delayed shipment of copper bracelets and the other a computer-generated solicitation for web services. Pulling a few dollars from her wallet, she headed next door.

Matteo was behind the counter, inserting a tray of miniature peanut butter pumpkins in the display case, a specialty he only made each October. He looked content to be back in his normal environment, yet had the rough edges of a man who'd clearly suffered a few sleepless nights.

"Good morning, Sadie." Matteo's attempt to sound like it was any ordinary day failed. He was too falsely chipper.

"Is it a good morning?" Sadie asked. She looked around to make sure the shop was empty before continuing. "I'm not sure it's a good idea for you to be open."

Matteo took a raspberry truffle out of the case and tossed it over the counter. Sadie caught it with the finesse of a major league catcher, but didn't fall for the diversion tactic.

"Thanks, but you're dodging the issue."

"There is no issue," Matteo said. "You said my prints weren't found anywhere, so there's no reason for me to hide. Not that there is, anyway, since I'm not guilty. Besides, I'm losing business by staying closed. And I have to keep my customers happy." He tossed another truffle at Sadie, this one pistachio cream.

"Well, I have to admit I'm glad you're not hiding behind counters anymore, but I wish you'd let someone run the shop for you, just for a few days, until this mess gets sorted out." Sadie paused. "Have you heard from Tina?"

"As a matter of fact, no," Matteo said. "Which strikes me as odd. With all this going on, I'd think she would call to let me know she's OK."

"Ah...then you don't know." Sadie did some quick thinking.

"Know what?" The concern on Matteo's face made Sadie wish she had better news.

"I'm sorry, Matteo, but it seems the police picked her up again. She called me last night from the jail." Sadie winced at the explosion she knew was coming.

"What? She called *you* last night? And didn't even call me? Why would she do that?"

"Maybe she didn't want to connect your phone number to the police station. She might have been trying to protect you." Sadie said. "She was only allowed one call. She knew I'd come talk to you. The town is small enough for the word of her arrest to have spread to Stefano and your family lawyer without Tina needing to call either of them. I figured she would be bailed out by now and would have called you."

"No, I haven't heard from her," Matteo said. "Or from our attorney, Nick Perry. I wonder if he's blinded by his affection for Luisa. I hear they've been dating since negotiations with Serrano-Flanagan ended. He's been a bit off his game since that whole disaster. He didn't say outright that he was in favor of our selling, and publicly appeared not to care either way, but I never thought he was objective enough."

"That's an interesting opinion. How does your mother feel about Nick?"

"She adores him, from what Tina has told me. She thinks he's about to become her fourth son. But I find it hard to believe that Luisa has gone that soft. Still, I haven't spoken to her directly in at least two years."

Sadie winced at this added proof that Matteo was left out in the cold when it came to his family. She thought about how alone he must feel, how vulnerable.

She surveyed the display case while mulling over this new information.

"Look, I don't need protecting," Matteo said, reading Sadie's thoughts.

"I'm not sure..." Sadie paused as a young woman entered, looked around and purchased an assortment of nuts and chews. While the customer continued to browse, Sadie stepped aside and moved to the end of the counter, where she picked up a culinary trade magazine. The publication amazed her with the multitude of merchandise, machinery and advertising opportunities displayed. She stopped flipping through pages when she came to an ad for a recent trade show. The blue and gold logo with a "C" in the center matched the pin in the photo Tina had shown her, the one found at the crime scene. Her hunch had been right. Matteo must have dropped the pin at the winery that night.

"I'm not sure it's true that you don't need protecting," Sadie continued after the woman left, filing away the information about the pin's origins for later analysis. "And, even if it is…Tina might think you do."

Matteo laughed. "Are you implying Tina might think *I* killed him? That's silly. Tina has known me since junior high. She would never think I'm capable of something that horrible."

"I didn't realize you'd known each other that long." Sadie looked over a plate of caramel turtles while waiting for Matteo to spill more information.

"Yes," Matteo said. "She moved to California from the Midwest when we were teenagers. Lived down the street from us. We even dated in high school for a while when I was a senior and she was a freshman."

Sadie frowned. "Well, that puts a different perspective on things."

"In what way?"

"In every way, Matteo." Sadie sighed, losing her patience. "There's obvious tension between Tina and Stefano, plus you and Tina seem pretty close, what with all the phone calls. Has Stefano shown signs of jealousy over the years?"

Matteo threw back his head and laughed. "You could say that. People talk about 'sore losers.' Stefano is a case study in 'sore winners.' Even though we both dated Tina, it was at different times. Obviously Stefano was the last man standing."

"Standing at the altar, you mean," Sadie clarified.

"Exactly. Tina could have married either one of us, but she chose Stefano."

"Sounds like you resent that," Sadie said.

"No, no, not at all. Tina is like a little sister to me now. I went off to culinary school, and Tina and Stefano spent the last three years of high school together. Stefano is the one who resents our closeness. He doesn't understand that men and women can be friends without romance. But it made sense they would end up a couple. Besides, things worked out for the best. I have my business here in the city and she has her Tremiato Napa lifestyle. "

"Maybe," Sadie said. She didn't comment on the wistful subtext she heard in Matteo's voice. It occurred to her that whether or not he was disappointed in Tina's choice of a husband, he must sometimes find his life lonely. "But the impression I get when I talk to Tina is that she's tired of the family politics."

"Who wouldn't be?" Matteo said. "Why do you think I'm here and not there?"

"To keep my chocolate supply constant?" Sadie smirked.

"That is my one and only reason," Matteo grinned. "Speaking of which, are you in the market for anything this morning, or is this just an interrogation?"

"I believe I have a craving for a double vanilla crème – no, make that two, please." Sadie placed several now-wrinkled dollar bills on the counter. After Matteo rang up the order and handed back her change, she returned to Flair.

* * *

As Sadie stepped into the store, she passed an exiting customer laden with several large Flair bags. Multiple purchases always set an optimistic tone for the day, and she smiled.

"Good sale?" Sadie asked Amber, who looked proud.

"Excellent sale," Amber replied. "Black satin pants, a beaded tunic, two lace camisoles in different colors, a cashmere sweater from the new arrivals section and a matching necklace-bracelet set."

"Nice job," Sadie said as she tossed Amber a double vanilla crème. "See? You don't even need me here."

A sharp yip from the velvet pillow signaled Coco's not-so-subtle demand for a treat, as well.

"Sorry, Coco," Sadie said. "No chocolate for you. Here's a nice, healthy treat," she said as she dug into a pocket and pulled out a tiny biscuit. She patted Coco's fuzzy head and scratched her behind the ears as the little dog ate, then turned back to Amber.

"It's not true that you're not needed here," Amber laughed. "Someone has to pay to restock this merchandise when it sells. Oh, you had a phone call. I left a message on your desk."

"Thanks. Anyone in particular?"

"No one I know. Just a woman who asked me to have you return her call. It's a 707 area code, if that helps," Amber said as Sadie headed for her office.

Sadie sat at her desk and picked up the message. As she already knew by the area code, it was from St. Vin, or somewhere in that general vicinity. It wasn't a stretch to assume it could be from the Tremiato Winery. Yet, to her knowledge, no one in the Tremiato family knew how to contact her except Tina. When she first arrived in wine country, she had purposely not handed out business cards to avoid revealing her connection to Matteo. And once her field trip turned into a murder investigation, she was more focused on listening than on advertising her role as amateur sleuth or fashion guru. She dialed the number and leaned back in her chair.

"Detective Shafer speaking."

The female detective's voice took Sadie by surprise. She'd been expecting Stefano or even Angelo, who could have gotten her number from Tina. She took a breath.

"This is Sadie Kramer." A straight business approach seemed best.

"Hello Ms. Kramer. Thank you so much for returning my call." The sound of shuffling papers crinkled through the phone line. "I'm working on the Tremiato Winery case, and I'm calling guests who stayed at The Vintage Vine recently. I believe you were there a few nights ago?"

"Yes. The night before the murder." *Why waste time mincing words*, Sadie figured. She already recognized the voice and name from the kitchen visit at the inn. Clearly the detectives had obtained a list of guests and contact information.

"We just have a few questions." More paper shuffling.

"Yes, how can I help you?" Sadie shifted in her chair, her investigative instincts giving her that familiar sense that she was standing on tiptoe looking into a forbidden box full of delicious information.

"Actually, we were hoping you might be able to come in; otherwise we can do this on the phone," Detective Shafer said. "You're the only guest at the inn that night who was also at the winery the following morning. Anything you saw or heard might be useful."

It occurred to Sadie for a fraction of a moment that the police might actually be considering her as a suspect. She shrugged off the thought. Even if she were a suspect, which was a ridiculous notion, listening to the detectives' questions and watching their behavior in person might offer her several clues that could help her to figure out who the murderer could be.

"How did you know I was at the winery that morning?" Her question probably ramped up the detective's suspicions, but Sadie was more interested in the answer than she was in proving her own innocence.

"Two of our uniforms said you came from the winery with platters of food." Shafer smiled. "They were pretty excited about those appetizers. I've never seen two grown men drool so openly over a plate of bruschetta."

Sadie's mind wandered toward the chocolate-drizzled cream puffs that Luisa had included in the mountain of food. Maybe there were more cream puffs waiting for her.

She paused. Although she'd just returned home the day before, she wasn't at all tired, and her adventurous blood was boiling in her veins. She decided to go for it.

"I'd be glad to come up," Sadie said. "Would tomorrow morning work? With traffic, I'm bound to get there late if I drive up today.

"Tomorrow morning is fine. We'll see you then." The line disconnected.

CHAPTER FIFTEEN

A typical San Francisco fog hovered around the Golden Gate Bridge the following morning and continued to surround Sadie as she headed up the 101 and into wine country. It weighed on her shoulders the way thoughts about the Tremiato case weighed on her mind. She fought to stay objective. It seemed impossible that Matteo could be guilty; nothing in her friendship all these years hinted at homicidal tendencies. *But is it always the one you least suspect?* And Tina was sweet...wasn't she? Stefano was more difficult to pinpoint. He'd seemed genuinely concerned about Tina when he'd spoken to her at The Grapevine. Yet to hear Tina tell it, he wasn't to be trusted. Although Sadie didn't believe Stefano was setting up his own wife to take the blame for murder, she couldn't be sure that he wasn't up to something. As for the other Tremiatos, they were mostly unknown elements. Elena was focused on family and tradition, and her age and seeming frailty – in Sadie's mind – put her out of the running as a murder suspect. Angelo seemed less inclined to indulge in the emotional turmoil than his brothers, but that outer calm might hide an inner drama queen. And Luisa was just a shadow of her mother. But maybe Luisa, tall and tough, was ready to emerge from the shadows; maybe Mr. Flanagan's demise somehow freed Luisa from the trap of having little to no power in her family.

The police station sat two blocks north of The Grapevine, reminding Sadie she might need to stop at the quaint cafe for another salad after meeting with the detectives. Maybe even a slice of their cheddar sourdough bread. And a glass of Tremiato Chardonnay. And something for dessert. And...

Her thoughts refocused as she pulled into the station's parking lot. Black and white patrol cars filled a row on one side, while spaces sat open for visitors on the other. She chose a spot, parked and turned off the engine. She pulled down the visor and glanced into the mirror, adjusting the jaunty peacock feather clip she'd snapped into her hair on impulse before she left that morning. She reached for her tote bag out of habit before remembering she'd left Coco with Amber. With all the attention Coco received from shop customers, the Yorkie would hardly miss Sadie. As much as she loved the dog, she'd move faster on her own this time, though Coco was a good listener. Still, she was determined to get as much information out of the trip as possible.

A low hum of activity greeted her as she entered the station. Wooden desks spread across an open room, reminding her of teachers' desks from school days. A few uniformed officers worked at computer screens while others talked on phones and scribbled notes. A woman holding the hand of a young child stood at the information counter. Sadie settled into a folding metal chair and waited for the woman to finish her business.

"Ms. Kramer?"

Sadie startled, not expecting to hear her name before she announced herself to the information clerk. Looking up, she noted the young, athletic woman who had spoken. Even without a name tag, she recognized the voice as that of Detective Shafer. Somehow the short brown hair and piercing blue eyes caught her by surprise. The detective looked sturdier than her voice, an observation that didn't even make sense as she took in the woman's slender stature.

"Yes," Sadie said, standing to shake the detective's outstretched hand.

"I appreciate you coming in," Detective Shafer said. "How was the drive?"

Sadie knew small talk when she heard it. It only served to heighten the feeling that this was a preface to a more serious talk. "Foggy, but fine."

"Yes, a classic San Francisco morning." Detective Shafer motioned to a hallway. "Why don't you come on back to our office? We just have a few questions about what you might have seen or heard on your last visit."

"Of course," Sadie said, feeling oddly guilty at being directed through a police station. What on earth had possessed her to wear black and white stripes that day? She touched the feathers in her hair for luck.

She followed the detective to an interview room similar to those she'd seen on television. The plain, functional room was neither welcoming nor foreboding. Sadie looked around before sitting down at a center table, somehow disappointed not to see any donuts.

A second detective joined them, closing the door behind him. Again, the absence of a nametag didn't keep Sadie from recognizing the officer as Detective Hudson. The tall, lanky man was identifiable as soon as he spoke. Sadie had always been good at remembering voices.

"Hello, Ms. Kramer, I'm Detective Hudson. Thank you for coming in."

The introductions seemed so formal until Sadie reminded herself that, while she'd witnessed their visit at the inn, they didn't know that. From their viewpoint, she was just someone on The Vintage Vine's guest list. She had an unfair advantage, which made her feel somewhat relieved. She sat up straighter and waited for the questions to begin. *Where were you the night of...*

"Ms. Kramer..." Detective Hudson paced as he began.

"Please call me Sadie. Unless I'm in trouble. Then you can call me Ms. Kramer. But I'm not in trouble, right?" *Holy marzipan, now I'm babbling.*

"You're not in any trouble, Ms. Kramer...Sadie." Sadie recognized the same soft tone that Detective Shafer had used when questioning Tina at the inn. Even her expression was softer than her partner's. *Good cop, bad cop?*

"We understand you run a shop next door to Cioccolata in San Francisco, Matteo's shop."

"Yes, that's right. I have a fashion boutique called Flair."

"And you just happened to be staying at The Vintage Vine the night of the murder, as well as attending the event at the Tremiato Winery the next morning. Was this a coincidence?" Detective Hudson stopped pacing and folded his arms across his chest as he asked the question.

Sadie leaned forward, resting her forearms on the table, her hands clasped. She'd seen this stance play out well on television. It was worth a try. "No, it wasn't a coincidence. You already know my boutique is next door to Cioccolata. I didn't just happen to be at his family's winery. I came up because he's a friend and I was concerned about him."

"Why?" Detective Shafer's voice was kinder.

"I was worried because I'd overheard an argument he was having on the phone the day before. I had gone over to buy some buttercreams because his are the best I've ever had. They're even better than the ones you can get from…"

"What kind of argument?" Detective Hudson asked.

"I'm not sure. I couldn't hear anything specific. But his tone of voice worried me." Sadie paused, thinking. "Actually, I do remember one thing he said."

"And what was that?"

"He said, 'You need to back off.'"

"Back off? Back off from what?"

"I have no idea. That was the only thing I heard. I'd tell you if I'd heard more." Sadie was a little puzzled by Detective Hudson's attitude. The interview felt more like an interrogation. Maybe she should have done this on the phone. Driving fatigue was making her feel prickly.

"Do you think he was being threatened?" Detective Shafer asked.

"Or maybe he was the one doing the threatening." Hudson interjected. "'You need to back off' sounds like a threat to me."

"No," Sadie said firmly. "That's not something Matteo would do. It would be completely out of character for him."

"Sometimes people go to extreme lengths when they're in crisis," Detective Shafer offered. "Maybe he got in over his head with the business deal somehow?"

"Or maybe you're just covering up for him." Again, Detective Hudson.

Sadie stood quickly and leaned forward, her ceramic zebra pendant landing on the desk with a crisp tap as she matched Detective Hudson's imposing stance. If she knew what sounds zebras made, she was sure the noise would replace her voice when she opened her mouth to speak. "Detective, I took an extra day off work to drive up here in good faith in case your department needed my help. I do *not* understand why you seem to be accusing me of 'aiding and abetting,' or whatever you call it."

Detective Shafer held up one hand to stop her partner from commenting any further and Sadie from blowing a gasket. "No one is accusing you of anything. And we're grateful for your time. Aren't we, Detective Hudson?"

"We are grateful, ma'am. We just get a little overzealous when someone is murdered in our town. Everyone's a suspect."

As Detective Hudson backed away from the table, Sadie sat back down. "I completely understand," Sadie said. She clutched the zebra in one fist and thanked it silently.

"Just a few more questions, if that's OK with you."

"Of course."

"Do you have any idea who Matteo was talking to during that phone call?"

Sadie shook her head. "No, not a clue."

"We believe he was talking to the victim. His phone records show numerous calls between Matteo's shop and the victim's office over the last few months."

"Wouldn't that make sense if they were negotiating a business deal?"

"Yes, but those negotiations were already over. The Tremiatos had decided not to sell. Yet the calls continued."

"I can't help you there," Sadie said. "Matteo never discussed any family matters with me. I always thought he was estranged from them." "Never" stopped at recent days, but Sadie didn't feel bound to reveal this, though she may have been more open if Detective Hudson had been less shrill.

"Other than the business dealings over the potential sale, it seems he *was* estranged. Did you know any of the other family members before coming up here this past weekend?"

Sadie shook her head. "No, only Matteo."

"Any impressions of the family during your visit?"

Sadie resisted the urge to say they were all completely wacko, in her opinion, settling instead on a safe understatement. "They seem to have a few issues." She was certain she saw Detective Shafer fight to hold back a smile.

"If you suspect Matteo, which is what it sounds like, why are you holding Tina?"

"Because the cork found in her kitchen has traces of broken glass, plus it's from a bottle of cabernet, the same type of wine found on the victim's body," Detective Hudson said.

"Well, I can see that wouldn't look good," Sadie said.

"Speaking of which...You stayed at The Vintage Vine the night before the murder." Detective Shafer paused to look down at her notes. "Actually, according to the medical examiner's report, the time of death was between 10 pm and midnight. So technically you stayed there the night *of* the murder."

"Yes."

"Did you ever see the innkeeper leave the inn?"

"No," Sadie said. "In fact, she was in the kitchen most of the evening, baking blueberry muffins for the next morning. They were delicious, I might add."

"About what time did you retire to your room?"

Sadie thought it over before answering. "Probably around 11 pm."

"So she easily could have gone out after you went to sleep."

"Objection. Calls for speculation."

The detectives and Sadie turned toward the unexpected voice, finding a man of medium height in the doorway. His light, but tan skin and blondish-brown hair reminded Sadie of surfers she saw on occasional visits to Santa Cruz. If he lost twenty pounds and twenty years, he could fit right in with that crowd.

"Counselor Perry," Detective Hudson said, circling the table and heading toward the doorway. "I don't recall anyone asking you to come in." Turning to Sadie, he added, "Is this man your lawyer?"

"Of course not!" Hearing the indignation in her voice, Sadie threw a quick apology toward the attorney. "No offense."

"None taken."

"Why would I need a lawyer?" Sadie asked.

"You don't need one. And Counselor Perry was just leaving." Detective Shafer stood and pointed to the door.

"Not so fast. The Tremiato family asked me to stop by to make sure Ms. Kramer was not being harassed. Besides, you're just still sore about the Morgan's Bar and Grill case." He faced Sadie directly and whispered, "Bogus health code violation." He held out his hand. "Nick Perry, attorney for the Tremiato family. Here at their request, *pro bono*."

Sadie's thoughts gathered like a sudden, swirling wind funnel. "How did the family even know I was coming up?"

"Word gets around."

Sadie looked at Mr. Perry for a moment trying to determine how open he might be to sharing information. This could work to her advantage, having direct contact with the Tremiato's lawyer. And if he wasn't going to charge for his services, so much the better. She and her zebra began to feel more cheerful.

"Well, maybe I do need a lawyer. If I'm going to continue being interrogated like this, I'd like him to stay." Sadie looked back and forth between the detectives. The sudden turn of events appeared to have them baffled.

"That won't be necessary," Detective Hudson said. "I think we've covered everything." He took a business card from his pocket and handed it to Sadie. "Just let us know if you think of anything else."

After a few words in parting, Sadie and the lawyer found themselves on the front steps of the police station.

"Well, that was all very odd," Sadie said.

"Yes, I'm sorry to barge in like that."

"No," Sadie continued. "Not you. I'm grateful you showed up. Their whole line of questioning was bizarre. I drove up to try to help out and ended up feeling like a suspect."

"Don't worry, that's how these cases are. They do have to look at all possibilities, so everyone's a suspect."

"Yes, that's what Detective Hudson said." Sadie thought back to a few other cases she'd handled where every person she met seemed to have something to hide and something to gain from the crime she investigated.

"And you were there, both the night before and that day at the winery," Nick continued.

"How do you know that?"

"Tina is my client, as are all Tremiato family members. We talk often."

"Of course," Sadie said. "Speaking of Tina, how is she?"

"She's holding up. I hope to have her out by tomorrow."

"But they found the cork from the broken wine bottle in her kitchen."

"Yes, but that's still circumstantial. There were no fingerprints on it, so her claim that it was planted is feasible."

"Well, that's promising," Sadie said. "She seems nice. She also thinks someone is trying to set her up. If there were no fingerprints, that would make sense, right? Otherwise hers would be on it?"

"Maybe, maybe not. Fingerprints can be wiped clean. Don't you watch TV at all?" A teasing grin crossed the lawyer's face.

"I'm more of a cooking show fan, personally," Sadie said. "How about you? Reality shows, maybe?"

"Hardly. I see far too much reality in this line of work. I stick to HGTV."

Nick's phone rang, and when he took the call, Sadie glanced at her watch. Her stomach rumbled, and she remembered that she'd promised herself a meal after the meeting with the detectives. Taking advantage of the chance to slip away, Sadie mouthed the words, "thank you," and headed for her car.

CHAPTER SIXTEEN

The Grapevine was crowded, as was to be expected at noon in a popular café. Sadie found a small table between a showcase of wooden boxes covered with shellacked wine labels and a chalkboard advertising the soup and sandwich special of the day. A young server with multiple piercings and fingernail polish of indefinable color greeted her almost immediately. Lost in an effort to read a tattoo on the twenty-something's wrist, Sadie merely pointed to the chalkboard and said, "I'll have this."

The single chair at the table promised a meal in solitude. A dull headache had started to form as soon as she left the police station's steps, as if every question the detectives asked had suddenly followed her, crept into her blood stream and started pounding on timpani. Her half-hidden table offered a chance to detox from the meeting in peace. She picked up her glass of water, took a sip and closed her eyes, willing her mind to be swept away to a Caribbean island, or anywhere devoid of detectives and dilemmas. She could almost feel the warm, soft sand on her bare feet, the sun on the bridge of her nose and a sweet breeze that smelled of coconut...or corn and jalapenos. *What? Corn and jalapeños?*

Sadie opened her eyes abruptly and looked down at her table, finding a bowl of chowder alongside a sandwich with melted cheese oozing out the sides. She looked up to find the young server staring at her curiously.

"What is this?"

"The lunch special. Turkey melt panini with jalapeño-corn chowder."

"Of course!" Sadie grinned at the server, which either satisfied the girl or scared her away. In either case, Sadie was left to enjoy her meal, which smelled better than a coconut-scented breeze. She wrapped her hands around the ciabatta bread and lifted it to her mouth, prepared to take a bite.

"Well, fancy meeting you here!"

Sadie lowered the sandwich and watched Stefano pull an extra chair from a nearby table. Within seconds he was seated across from her, helping himself to a few sweet potato fries.

Sadie pulled her lunch a little closer to her, hoping to save a few fries for herself.

"I'm here to pick up my usual Reuben, with extra sauerkraut. I've always been fond of a good Reuben, and The Grapevine makes the best. I call in an order at least twice a week." Stefano leaned back in his chair and scanned the room. Sadie was certain she saw him wink at two attractive women at a nearby table. *Hardly subtle.*

"And what brings you back to our town so soon?"

There was no question Stefano was fishing for answers. Sadie debated her best course of action and decided to be direct.

"I came up to meet with the detectives working on Tina's case."

"You came all the way up here to meet with them?" Stefano tapped his fingers on the table. The gesture struck Sadie as more nervous than casual.

"Yes, they asked me to."

Stefano raised his eyebrows. "Whatever for?

"I suppose to answer questions about anything I noticed that morning at the winery, as well as the nights I stayed at the inn. But they didn't get to all their questions because Mr. Perry 'rescued' me, I thought because one of the Tremiatos had sent him. Was it you?"

"I didn't know you were here until Angelo told me, and I think he heard from Luisa. Or … I don't know. Word gets around."

The server who had waited on Sadie set a bag in front of Stefano, who thanked her with one of his obviously famous smiles. The young woman responded to his flirtation with a frown before walking away.

Sadie took a bite of the turkey melt, and then ate a spoonful of soup, savoring the combination of flavors.

"I guess I can't charm everyone," Stefano sighed and returned his attention to Sadie. "But tell me, did you think of anything to tell the detectives that might help Tina? I can't stand to see her going through this. Does she seem like someone who'd be capable of murder?"

"I don't think so," Sadie said. "But you know her better than I do. Do you think there's any chance she could have done it?"

"Of course not," Stefano said, quickly, as if he'd set up the question specifically so he could answer it. "Then you have to help get her out of this. You were there at the inn the night Flanagan was killed. Surely Tina was home that whole night?" Stefano's tone was anxious.

"Yes, I was at the inn. I watched her bake muffins and heard her talking with guests in the evening. But I did go to bed at some point. I didn't have her in sight all night. I didn't have any reason to think I needed to keep watch over her then. Hopefully the police will find out enough information that they'll direct their search elsewhere."

"But the cork was found there," Stefano added.

"Yes, and that brings up an interesting point," Sadie said. "The detectives didn't find it during the first search, only later, after they received an anonymous tip. What does that tell you?"

"That it wasn't there the first time."

"Right, unless they missed it," Sadie pointed out. "But that's unlikely. My guess is that it was planted there."

Stefano remained quiet, his expression unreadable. Finally, he spoke. "You think someone is trying to frame her?"

Sadie nodded. "That's the only explanation I can see. Or someone is trying to throw the police off *their* trail."

"But who would want to do that?" Stefano looked genuinely baffled, but Sadie found herself wondering if it was an act. Something about his tone seemed odd. *Stress? Confusion? Guilt?*

"I don't know, Stefano. I don't know her circle of friends and acquaintances, but you do. Can you think of anyone who might have a motive for framing your wife? Someone she wronged or someone who's angry?" *Or maybe someone who's jealous?*

"No," Stefano said firmly. "Tina doesn't have any enemies."

Sadie tried a different angle before launching into her lunch again. The more information she could obtain the better. There was always a chance Stefano would reveal something he didn't mean to.

"How about the sale of the winery? What can you tell me about that?"

"What do you mean? There wasn't any sale." Stefano said curtly, which made Sadie wonder if he were bitter because the proposed sale didn't end the way he wanted it to.

"You don't sound happy about that. I take it you were in favor of selling."

"Not at first," Stefano admitted. "Like everyone in our family, I'm proud of what we've built up over generations. But when Flanagan came to us and explained the proposed changes that Serrano-Flanagan had in mind, it made sense. We don't have the capital to stay up with the new technology and marketing. Other wineries are expanding, adding events, even hosting concerts. It makes sense to do what's needed to stay up with the times, and the sale would have enabled the winery to catch up. In addition, our income is down because other wineries now have more draw with all their bells and whistles. And it's harder to run with our father gone. Once Flanagan pointed out the benefits of selling, it made sense to me."

"What about your lawyer, Nick Perry? Did he have an opinion?"

"Not really," Stefano said. "He's pretty good at staying objective. He let Flanagan work out the offer and made sure we knew we could counter with a different proposal. Nick just helped us with the details. You know, explained how the sale would take place, what paperwork would be needed, what we would be paid, how the money would be transferred, that type of thing."

"Sounds about right," Sadie said. "It sounds like he did the job of a good, objective attorney and represented your family in the decision about this sale."

"He handled it well," Stefano said. "Lawyers can be annoying, but he's a good guy. We've had lunch on occasion, and he's stopped by the store a few times. I don't think Angelo is thrilled that Nick is dating our sister, but I think he's been good for her."

"Were Nick and your sister dating during the negotiations with Serrano-Flanagan?"

"No. They didn't start seeing each other until all those disastrous meetings finally ended. I'm actually surprised he kept coming around. We would have scared off anyone else."

Sadie watched a young couple pick up a bagged order, pay and exit the café. She was beginning to wish Stefano would leave, as well. She wasn't getting much information out of him, plus her soup was getting cold.

As if he'd read her mind, Stefano stood up. "I'd better get back to the store and let you finish your lunch in peace. It's been a pleasure." He turned away, then paused and faced Sadie again. "There's something that's been bugging me. Why was Tina even in the fermentation building that morning? Wasn't she at the inn, serving breakfast? You were there. You must have seen her."

Sadie paused before answering. It seemed an odd question coming from Stefano, who surely must have asked Tina the same thing.

"Yes, she served breakfast," Sadie said. "And a delicious one, at that. But she got a phone call as we were finishing up and said she needed to run a quick errand. It's my understanding that Luisa called and asked her to help with something. I've been wondering about this since I get the feeling she and Luisa don't have the best of relationships."

"You're right about that," Stefano said. "I've never understood why Luisa didn't take to Tina. She was cold to her right from the start, when I started dating her. Maybe Luisa resents Tina joining the family? I don't know. I gave up trying to figure that out a long time ago. Luisa's always been a bit of a cold fish, even when we were growing up."

On that note, Stefano left the café, sporting another of his dazzling smiles as he held the front door open for two elderly women on their way in. Sadie had to give him credit. At least he was an equal opportunity flirt.

CHAPTER SEVENTEEN

Fortified with a good meal and the sense that the Tremiatos were on the verge of telling her what she wanted to know, Sadie headed, once again, for the winery. As she expected, Angelo was behind the counter in the tasting room. He didn't seem at all surprised to see her. Sadie wondered if Stefano had called him to confirm that she was back in town, and if he had, she wondered why.

Luisa and Elena were nowhere to be seen. Other than two tourists sipping wine at the counter, Angelo was alone.

"Back for another sample of our chardonnay?" Angelo approached Sadie with a wine glass and bottle, but Sadie shook her head.

"I'm driving back to the city in a bit, but I'd love a glass of water, if it's not a bother."

"No bother at all," Angelo said. His tone was polite but reserved. He brought out a bottle of imported sparkling water from beneath the counter and filled the wine glass, adding a twist of lemon. "I understand the police called you in for questioning?"

"Ah, Stefano must have called you."

"Yes, he said he saw you at The Grapevine."

"Indeed he did," Sadie said, curious to see if Angelo was trying to pry information from her?

"I suppose that makes sense the police would want to talk to you," Angelo said. "After all, you were here the afternoon before the murder and the morning after."

He makes it sound like he thinks I'm a suspect! Sadie thought.

"I actually volunteered to drive up to allow them to interview me in person," Sadie said. "Sometimes it helps investigators to get an outside opinion." Sadie immediately wondered if the statement was a mistake. Did it sound like she was implying a family member was responsible for the murder? Though clearly the most likely possibility, hinting at it did seem disrespectful, if not downright dangerous. After all, one dead body had already shown up on the property. Sadie wasn't eager to have another one show up, especially hers.

Luisa emerged from the back room, carrying a stack of paperwork. She nodded to Sadie, a quasi-smile on her face. Sadie suspected it was the full extent of enthusiasm that the sole female sibling ever showed.

"What brings you back to town?" Luisa's question struck Sadie as essentially rhetorical, yet in need of an answer for the sake of courtesy.

"The detectives on the murder investigation wanted to ask me a few questions," Sadie explained, though she had a hunch Luisa already knew that.

"Your boutique in San Francisco is next door to our brother's chocolate shop."

Luisa's comment took Sadie by surprise, as did the subtle glance between brother and sister that followed it.

"Yes, that's right," Sadie said. At this point, it seemed best to be upfront with the Tremiatos.

"You didn't mention that when you were here before."

"It didn't come up," Sadie replied. "I was here to get away, to sample some good wines and spend time in the country. My focus wasn't on my boutique." It wasn't a lie. Granted, she'd never offered that information outright. But they'd never asked her directly.

"Then you know about the sale," Luisa said. "Well, the sale that fell through. Matteo must have mentioned that to you."

"Actually, no," Sadie said. "I didn't know about that until I read about it in the paper. My friendship with Matteo mostly involves our relationship as neighbors and business owners, and he's never shared much personal information. I was only vaguely aware that his family even owned a winery."

"That sounds like Matteo," Luisa said. "Always off in his own world."

"He does love what he's doing," Sadie offered, a gentle defense of her friend.

"Well, that's nice for him," Luisa said.

Nothing in her voice hit Sadie as sincere.

"Our mother was furious that Matteo was willing to sell," Luisa added.

"Stefano told me he was also willing to sell at first. Was she upset with him?" Sadie was sure Luisa would defend Stefano somehow, a direct contrast to the attitude toward Matteo.

"That was different," Luisa said. "He was just looking out for our mother's best interests." Quite the contrast from her attitude toward Matteo, but not a surprising one.

"Wasn't that what Matteo was doing?" Some unexpected sense of fortitude, or perhaps loyalty to her friend, encouraged Sadie to push for more explanation.

"No," Luisa said firmly. "Matteo has never cared about this family. If he had, he'd have stayed here to help run the winery. Instead he chose to run off and make *candy*."

Ah, Sadie thought. *So chocolate is frivolous?*

"Have you ever *tried* his chocolate?" Sadie asked. "It's quite remarkable. Customers line up out the door for it. His raspberry truffles, for example, simply melt in…"

"No. And I don't care to," Luisa said, cutting Sadie off. "I've never been fond of chocolate, anyway."

"Yet you carry it here in your gift section," Sadie pointed out.

"Yes, because other people *are* fond of it. It's good business."

"But you don't carry Matteo's chocolates, which are popular at many gourmet shops." Sadie watched as color began to flood Luisa's cheeks. Just as she hoped, she was breaking through the woman's icy surface.

"Of course not!" Luisa snapped, then lowered her voice as the other customers turned their heads. "Why should we support him when he won't even support his own family?"

Sadie took a sip of sparkling water and changed the subject. "I suspect your lawyer leaned in the direction of selling, though he did a good job of laying out objective information. At least that's what Stefano said when I saw him at The Grapevine."

"Nick isn't a high-pressure type of man," Luisa said, her voice softening a bit. "Flanagan was the one who was pushy. He shouldn't have even been in sales, not with that attitude. He almost acted desperate to get us to sell, like an overly aggressive used car salesman."

Sadie had to agree with this. She'd always disliked sales reps who pressured her to bring their clothing or accessory lines into her boutique. Sometimes she even turned down items she might have otherwise carried just because the sales rep turned her off.

"Well, lawyers do like to get those legal fees, you know. A big sale could mean a good commission." Sadie watched as Luisa thought about her response.

Luisa shook her head. "Nick's not like that. He's already well to do. He represents half the wineries and restaurants in this area. He's an excellent lawyer who comes from a family full of lawyers. His motivation isn't money. He's dedicated to giving his clients the best possible representation."

Spoken like a person in love, Sadie thought.

"So he followed in his family's footsteps, like any good son would," Sadie said.

"Exactly," Luisa replied. "Or any good daughter, for that matter. Nick's parents wanted his older sister to go into law, as well. Instead she went into show biz. His parents were very disappointed. I would never do that to our family."

"No, I can see that," Sadie said, pausing. "What about Tina?"

"What about her?"

"She's a Tremiato," Sadie offered. "But she doesn't help here at the winery, does she?"

"Tina is not a Tremiato." Luisa's voice was firm.

"She married into your family."

"Exactly. Just because her name changed doesn't make her one of us." Luisa sighed, seeming tired. She moved down the counter to help Angelo set up glasses for a group of eight people who had just entered.

Since both Luisa and Angelo were busy, Sadie browsed the gift area. While admiring a set of corkboard coasters, she pondered whether any of the Tremiatos, other than Matteo, were happy with anything at all, including each other. Other than Stefano's flirtatious grins, had she ever seen any of them sport a sincere smile? Or speak kindly – as opposed to defensively – about each other? It almost felt as if the family were some type of club, that they felt they had to stick together, whether they wanted to or not. Yet they were quick to cast people out, at least the sister was. In Luisa's view, Matteo was out, Tina was out, and anyone who stood up against the family traditions in the future would likely be out, as well.

Sadie set the coasters down and moved along the row of gift items. Pausing by the back door she looked across the grounds to the main farmhouse, noting Elena seated on the porch, hands folded in her lap. The woman stared out across rows of grapevines. *If only I could read her thoughts*, Sadie thought. *I'll bet she knows more than she lets on.*

Three more customers entered the tasting room. Angelo greeted them while Luisa continued helping the party of eight. Without a clear reason to linger, Sadie waved goodbye and left.

CHAPTER EIGHTEEN

Coco sat properly, only her eyes darting back and forth, following the trail of a tiny peanut butter bone.

"You're the only one I can talk to about this, you know."

Sadie waved the dog treat in the air like an orchestra conductor, oblivious to the fact it was driving her sole audience member crazy. Sadie had always talked with her hands; it was part of her flamboyant personality. It would be impossible to analyze the Tremiato case aloud without some animated gestures.

"For example, Tina found poor Mr. Flanagan's body, but he died hours before she discovered him. Unless she snuck out the night before, after baking those delicious muffins, she's not the killer. There's no real evidence that she was, other than a silly cork that doesn't even have her fingerprints on it. And I'm quite sure that odd guest, Mr. Collins, planted it. But did Stefano set that up? Tina really had no motive. She'd never interacted with Flanagan and she didn't care one way or the other about the sale. In any case, she had no say in the matter."

Sadie paused just long enough for Coco to crane her neck, her tiny mouth opening and closing. Sadie resumed deliberations quickly and, therefore, her arm movements, and the bone continued to elude the poor dog. Coco sat down to wait out another round of debate.

"Whether or not Stefano is trying to make it look like Tina did it is another story altogether. But he had no beef with Mr. Flanagan, other than finding him annoying, I assume. If Stefano did the killing, I would think it was Matteo he would have been trying to confront. A crime of passion could certainly be fueled by jealousy. Was he jealous enough to commit murder? And killed Mr. Flanagan by accident, mistaking him for Matteo in the dark? It's a stretch, don't you think, Coco?"

A yip in return brought Sadie's gaze down to see Coco staring at her, wide eyed.

"Oh, Coco! You poor thing! I've been torturing you with this biscuit!" She stooped down and gave Coco the well-deserved peanut butter bone. To apologize further, Sadie adjusted the pink iPod shuffle on Coco's collar to a salsa playlist and gave her a second treat. Returning to her deliberations, Sadie watched Coco trot off with steps that she'd long ago labeled the Yorkie Samba.

Over a glass of merlot, Sadie reviewed other possibilities. She was fighting hard to dismiss Matteo as a suspect, but she couldn't rule him out completely. He'd already admitted going to meet Flanagan after the phone call that Sadie overhead. Perhaps Flanagan wasn't already dead when Matteo arrived, and they *did* meet. An argument may have ensued, ending up out of control. Maybe they struggled and Matteo was forced to protect himself, but with terrible consequences. Was it a matter of self-defense and then panic on Matteo's part? Like it or not, she had to admit it was possible.

Still, there were numerous clues that had yet to tie together. The cork in Tina's kitchen cupboard, for example. The pin that Detectives Hudson and Shafer had found at the crime scene. The mysterious Mr. Collins' visit to and quick vanishing from the inn. All the cell phone calls between Matteo and Mr. Flanagan. Behind all these varied factors was one consistent story. It was just a matter of discovering what it was.

"What's the common denominator, Coco? What one factor ties all these separate clues together?"

Coco did an amusing canine pirouette upon hearing her name. She yipped twice, though Sadie knew it was a ploy for another treat, not a solution to the murder.

"Yes, Coco. My mind is spinning, too."

The one direction she was hoping to avoid was the idea that Mr. Collins could be the killer. If this were true, it could leave the case unsolved. And Sadie hated loose ends. Mr. Collins could have committed the crime, planted the cork to make it look family related, and left town without a trail. While the family crumbled into turmoil, the killer would have run free. It could be as simple as that, not any type of family feud at all. As much as she hated the idea of finding out someone in Matteo's family was guilty – or, heaven forbid, Matteo himself – she knew that an unsolved murder would be harder on everyone involved.

Sadie started to pour another half glass of wine, then changed her mind and fixed a cup of peppermint tea, instead. Better to stay focused. Besides, she had a new hunch. Moving to her home office area, she settled in at her desk and fired up her computer. Coco followed, curling up on a plush throw rug beside the desk. Sadie leaned down and switched the iPod's music from salsa to a soothing blend of piano and flute solos. As Coco drifted off to sleep, Sadie took a trip into cyberspace.

The thought of doing a background check on the company that tried to acquire the Tremiato winery had crossed her mind before, but she'd dismissed it in favor of following evidence in front of her. Pondering the miscellaneous clues had brought a new question to mind. Was there something about the company that was rearing its ugly head now? Was this the common link?

What an amazing age of technology, Sadie mused as she ran some online searches on Serrano-Flanagan. Years ago, she'd have headed to the library, checked micro fiche, or even consulted with private investigators to dig up information on people or companies. Now she could just tap questions into a keyboard. Wearing fuzzy slippers and polka dot pajamas, no less!

Sadie plugged away at research for thirty minutes or so, finding nothing out of the ordinary. The company website was well designed, with links to businesses it had acquired. One by one, Sadie clicked through to check out each acquisition in the Napa Valley area, reading their basic information – location, wine specialties, and upcoming events – and paying particular attention to any "News" sections. It was clear that Serrano-Flanagan had invested in each business acquisition. To their credit, they had followed through on promises of improvement, upgrading equipment, spending generously on re-branding, and building new facilities such as fine dining establishments and even, in one case, a concert venue. Testimonies from regular customers made it clear the local community embraced the changes, though a few established wineries felt the progress diminished the historical aspects of the wine-making business. Serrano-Flanagan was a legitimate company.

Taking another approach, Sadie began to research the company's origins. Formed in 1997, Serrano-Flanagan was a subsidiary of a larger Boston company, PSF Enterprises, whose history dated back to the 1920s. Strictly an investment firm, PSF was parent to smaller companies that managed mergers and acquisitions in numerous areas. Their website was similar to that of Serrano-Flanagan, linking to companies around the country.

"Nothing strange about this that I can see, Coco," Sadie announced, causing Coco to stir from a brief nap. Coco responded with a slow canine yawn, lowered her head again and closed her eyes.

"But…" Sadie added, clicking the computer mouse several more times. "These companies are pretty new compared to the parent company. And I can't find any information about PSF company activities before these subsidiaries were formed. What do you think that's about?"

Getting nothing from the snoring Yorkie, Sadie fixed another cup of tea and checked the clock on her kitchen wall. It was still early enough to make a phone call. She returned to the living room, set down the tea, picked up her cell phone and dialed a number. Disappointed to reach voicemail, she left a stern message.

"Matteo, it's Sadie. We need to talk as soon as you get this. It's important. Come by my house when you can. I'll be up."

CHAPTER NINETEEN

Sadie opened the front door to find Matteo standing on the welcome mat, looking like a school child waiting to see the principal at the end of the day. She knew he'd interpreted her tone correctly when he'd listened to the voicemail. She expected him to tell the truth even if the truth made him squirm.

"Come in. Sit down."

Closing the door, she watched Matteo cross the room to the couch, where he sat. He bounced back up immediately when the couch squeaked at him. Reaching underneath a cushion, he pulled out a fist-sized object. He held it up, his eyebrows raised.

"That's Alfred. A prize from the last Canine Carnival," Sadie explained simply, as if all decent households kept red rubber hedgehogs under their couch cushions.

Matteo dropped the toy on the floor, sat back down and waited.

"Matteo," Sadie said, sitting down across from him. "I really want to help you, especially since you decided to ask for my help. When I first started worrying about you, I chose to visit your family winery. After the murder, I began to dig deeper, and when you told me you were in trouble, I returned to the area, spoke with your brothers, sister, and sister-in-law, observed your mother, agreed to return to speak with the police in person, and suffered countless lapses in chocolate consumption, all for your benefit. But I've hit a wall, and the only way I can get you out of this mess is if you level with me and tell me everything, even things you may not know you know. Tell me every last detail, Matteo. Anything you left out from the start even if you don't think it's important. There's got to be more than you told me."

Matteo sighed. "I wasn't trying to keep anything from you. I just thought you could figure out who killed Flanagan without having to get wrapped up in the whole story.

Especially when I knew you were up there at the winery already. It was safer for you that way. I stumbled across a bit of nastiness, and I didn't want to involve you."

"Well now I'm here and safe, and not there and possibly in some kind of peril. Help me out. Look." Sadie motioned to the computer and had Matteo follow her over. She pulled up the Serrano-Flanagan website. "Did you research this company when you were considering their offer to buy your family's winery?"

Matteo nodded. "Yes, I did. I'm sure my brothers did, too. I didn't want a company to take over the winery and let it fall apart, not after all the generations of work our family has put in to build its reputation. But, as you can see, they've done some great things with the other wineries they've bought. That was one of the things Flanagan stressed. That we'd be proud of the direction the winery would go under the ownership of Serrano-Flanagan. They did have a proven track record of following through with promises they made to other wineries in the area."

"Yet you decided not to go through with the sale," Sadie pointed out.

"Right. In the end, I felt the family legacy meant more to my mother than either the money from the sale or the promised improvements. Selling would have meant going against what my mother really wanted. It was more important to respect her wishes."

"You didn't get any hesitant feelings about the Serrano-Flanagan company itself?"

"No. I'm guessing you've seen their website and the websites of all the wineries they've acquired. There's nothing to indicate they aren't legitimate. They've always paid a generous amount for the purchase and each winery is more profitable now than before. I spoke with several wineries that had sold to them already, and they were all pleased. There was no reason to doubt Serrano-Flanagan's claim that they could do just as well for us. It just wasn't the right situation for our family."

"So why did you agree to meet Flanagan if you'd already decided not to sell? Tell me every detail. Something you think isn't important might be crucial. The police are going to pin the murder on someone, most likely someone in your family. If not Tina, then maybe Stefano, or it could even come back to you. You had the most business dealings with the victim. They might decide you wiped off the fingerprints yourself and then decided to let them go after Tina."

"I would never do that to Tina. Are you implying I would?" Matteo began to pace, kicking aside the red rubber hedgehog as he crossed the room. Coco raised her head from her comfortable cushion and gave Matteo her own version of the evil eye.

"No, no, dear boy! I'm just trying to look at everything as if I were with the police, and they are already scrutinizing everyone in your family. Please don't take your frustrations out on poor Alfred. You've upset Coco."

"Sorry," Matteo mumbled. "This never would have happened if Flanagan had just backed off," Matteo said. "But he kept pushing and pushing. Even after I gave him a firm answer, saying we would not be selling, he continued to pressure me. I told him to leave us alone, but he wouldn't."

"Well, that could give you motive, or ... did Flanagan *have* something on you, Matteo?"

His face paled. "No, of course not! I'm a man without secrets." Sadie wasn't quite sure she believed him, but she continued as if she did.

"Explain what led up to the meeting at the winery. You had information for him, right?"

Matteo sat down on the couch and ran his fingers through his hair. "About a week before I went back home, Flanagan called me, practically in hysterics. He apologized for being so pushy, but said he was being pressured from inside Serrano-Flanagan to force the sale through. According to Flanagan, someone high up in the company was blackmailing him."

"Who was it?"

"He wouldn't say. He just said the person had evidence that Flanagan's father had embezzled money from the parent company years ago, back in Boston. If he didn't get the Tremiato sale to go through, they were going to make it public."

"So he wanted to protect his family reputation?"

Matteo nodded, but then shook his head. "Yes, but that wasn't all. He also feared for his life, saying the Serrano family was long rumored to be well connected, if you know what I mean."

"I'm following you, Matteo. I've seen *The Godfather*."

"He didn't have any proof, of course, but he was scared."

"That's understandable," Sadie said. "So then what happened?"

"I wasn't going to sell the winery just to get him off the hook, though he pleaded with me to do exactly that. But I told him I'd do some checking to see if there was any truth to the accusations against his father. I told him to give me a few days to see what I could dig up."

Sadie frowned. "I've been searching online for anything that looked odd about the parent company, PSF Enterprises, since Serrano-Flanagan looks clean. But there's not a lot, other than the fact the company started up in the 1920s. There were some rumors of illegal dealings, but nothing that was ever substantiated."

"That's all I found, too," Matteo said. "So I hired a private investigator from Boston."

"You're kidding me, right? And this is the first you're telling me?"

"I told you from the start that I went to meet Flanagan to give him some information. I just didn't tell you what that information was. I didn't think it was important at that time. And I panicked, OK? I went to meet him, found him dead, and panicked. I wasn't thinking clearly about anything. That was a terrible shock."

"I know it must have been. But go on," Sadie said.

"The private investigator found some information on the Serrano side of the company. I told Flanagan that I had information that could get him off the hook with whoever was pressuring him from inside the company. He told me he was in the area near the Tremiato winery doing other business, so we agreed to meet in the fermentation building at midnight, a good time to avoid other people. But if anyone had caught us, I could have just said I wanted to visit to see how everyone in the family was doing, you know, big brother stuff. You know the rest of how that meeting went. Or didn't, I should say."

"What was the information you planned to give him, Matteo?"

"That it was the Serrano side of the company that embezzled the money. Flanagan's father wasn't involved."

"So you decided to meet at the winery to pass on this information...because you didn't want to talk over the phone?"

"Exactly. Everything the private investigator reported back to me supported Flanagan's claim that the Serrano family was connected. If true, they might have been bugging our phone calls all along. I wasn't going to risk that. And I didn't want him coming near my own business. I just wanted him to back off with the sales pressure. I thought he might be willing to drop it if he knew the company's blackmail claims had no basis."

"Who do you think was blackmailing Flanagan?"

"I can't be sure, but I suspect it was John Serrano, who runs the Serrano-Flanagan company in Sacramento. He would have been the only one above Flanagan who could manipulate him that way. The Serranos always had a slightly higher share in PSF Enterprises, right from the beginning."

"An Italian advantage over the Irish half of the company?"

"Yes," Matteo said, contemplating Sadie's statement.

"That's interesting," Sadie said. "PSF Enterprises was formed in the 1920s in Boston. There was a heavy Irish presence there at that time. And a lot of Italian-Irish rivalry. If you think about it, it seems odd that a business alliance between the Serranos and Flanagans would have even formed. But I guess greed can conquer other factors, even rivalry. They must have been making some good money. And you know what illegal business was lucrative at that time?"

Matteo answered immediately. "Bootlegging."

"Exactly," Sadie said. "I have a feeling corruption goes way back in this company. The question now is what's playing out currently.

CHAPTER TWENTY

A light mist greeted Sadie in the morning as she headed to Flair. She'd left home early to get to her office before Amber arrived to open the shop so that she could do some discreet investigating. Sleep had been elusive, anyway, as her mind tumbled the new, disjointed pieces of information around like clothes in a dryer. Tossing back and forth until Coco yipped with impatience from the lower edge of the bedspread, she finally got up, made coffee, dressed and headed out.

The time difference between San Francisco and Boston worked in her favor. She'd pried the phone number of the private detective Matteo had used out of him before he left the night before. If the P.I. had been able to unearth enough information for Matteo to approach Flanagan, he could probably obtain additional facts. Or spill them, if he already knew more than he'd told Matteo. Even unsubstantiated rumors could help at this point. Connecting the dots might be all it took to get to the bottom of things.

Sadie unlocked the door to Flair and relocked it from the inside. Heading to the back, she almost tripped over a stack of boxes that UPS had delivered the afternoon before. Amber certainly had her work cut out for her today. This was a good thing, since Sadie had plenty on her calendar, as well. The rescheduled Harvest Festival was only one day away, and she was determined to have the background information on Serrano-Flanagan before the event.

Setting up a pot of coffee, she flipped the switch on and settled in at her desk, jotting a few notes down before picking up the phone.

"Sal's Agency." The voice on the other end of the phone was rough with a heavy Boston accent. Sadie noted that, just as in the paper Matteo had given her, no last name was used. She wasn't sure whether this should encourage or dissuade her.

"Hello, Sal," Sadie began. "A friend and neighbor of mine, Matteo Tremiato, gave me your number. I'm working on a murder case here in California and wonder if I could ask you a few questions."

"Sure, doll. I'll tell you what I know. And for a pretty fee – negotiable, of course – I'll find you even more." A pause. "Wait a minute. Did you say murder case? I don't handle anything that has to do with murder. Too many hidden agendas and unknowns. I'm just a fact finder. You know, like a university researcher. But in a non-academic setting." The sound of a freight train in the background accentuated his point.

"I understand," Sadie said. "The information I'm looking for doesn't pertain directly to the murder. I just need facts, background stuff."

"In that case, what can I do for you?"

"I'm looking for some history on a company – PSF Enterprises, to be precise." Sadie waited patiently through the silence on the other end of the line.

"You know, I'm not familiar with a company by that name," Sal answered. "I probably can't help you, but I'll give you a call if a business with that name turns up." The call disconnected. Had Matteo not warned Sadie to expect this, she would have been frustrated or discouraged. Instead she waited for the expected return call, which came in around fifteen minutes later.

"Sorry about that," Sal said when Sadie answered. "Had a bad connection or somethin'. This is better." Not surprisingly, the number didn't match the one she had dialed.

"I was asking about PSF Enterprises," Sadie said. "I believe they're the parent company to Serrano-Flanagan?"

"Technically, yes," Sal said. "But they don't do much anymore. They used to be big back in the day here in Boston. But they're nothing more than an office now. They cut down operations here when they started opening up companies in other areas, like that one you have out there in California."

"To put all their focus on those subsidiaries?"

"You might say that. Or you could say it was to take focus off past operations in Boston."

"What kind of operations?" Sadie waited, pen in hand to take notes, if needed.

Sal laughed. "From the start, they weren't a reputable company. They weren't the only ones, of course. Plenty of illicit firms popped up around Prohibition. There was dough for the taking back then, everywhere. PSF Enterprises was set up as a transport company. And transport they did – from here to Canada and back. Oh, the Irish side of the company had a few deals going on down at the docks. But a couple of people got nabbed and that fizzled out pretty quick."

"Then what? Prohibition ended," Sadie pointed out.

"Yeah, but they had enough legitimate angles going to stay in business. I think the Italian side of the company stayed out of trouble for a few decades. The Irish side got caught up with fixing horse races for a while during the 60s and 70s. But they must have paid people off, because they never got caught. Then again, maybe those were rumors."

"What about embezzlement?"

"Ah, there's your real question, doll. That happened around the 80s. Money came up missing and both sides of the company pointed to the other. Nothing was ever proven on either side. The Flanagan side took the brunt of accusations, since they'd been the ones fixing the races not long before. And Joseph Flanagan was in charge of the accounting department, so it made sense to point to him. But no one proved anything. My inside sources say the Serrano side was behind it all. They made some big outside investments about the time the money disappeared. But they had paper trails to back them up. From here to Switzerland, I should say."

"Joseph Flanagan stayed with the company?"

"Yeah, once there was no proof that he was involved, and the scandal died down. He stayed until he died about ten years ago. His son now works at Serrano-Flanagan in Sacramento. You already know that, obviously, or you wouldn't have called me."

"Well," Sadie stalled. "I guess you haven't heard. You need to change that to past tense. Simon Flanagan is the one who was murdered last Saturday."

After a moment of silence, the investigator said, "I'm truly sorry to hear that. You know, you might consider leaving this whole thing alone. That company has always been mired in controversy."

"So it seems," Sadie said.

"Anyway, that's all I know," Sal continued. "And I suggest you lose this number."

That won't be hard, since it said it was blocked, Sadie thought.

"Wait, one more question," Sadie asked quickly, before Sal hung up. "The company name...PSF Enterprises...What was the "P" for? Was there a third partner?"

"No, there were only two partners, but..."

Sadie barely caught the rest of the answer before the line went dead.

* * *

Amber arrived promptly at 9:45 a.m., ready to set up the register and get the shop open for the day. She was surprised to find her employer already in the back office, doodling exotic flowers along the edge of a full sheet of scribbled notes.

"Early morning?" Amber asked.

"Couldn't sleep," Sadie replied, a safe answer that also happened to be true.

"You doodle like that when your brain's in overdrive," Amber pointed out. What Amber didn't know was that Sadie doodled like this when she was on the edge of putting the last pieces of a puzzle together. And this particular case was indeed a puzzle.

"We should price items for this weekend's Fall Clearance sale," Sadie said, putting her pen down. "All scarves and accessories need to be marked down. Those lace leggings that haven't been selling should go on clearance. And speaking of the clearance section…" Sadie stood up and walked out to the back area of the shop. "Let's take all the final sale items down another twenty percent. And we should put a few brighter orange and yellow items in the front display window, along with sale signs that will be delivered this afternoon. That should help draw customers in."

"I can do the mark-downs and rearrange the window this morning. I'll add the sale signs when they come in later." Amber said. "We have ads in the paper for this weekend, don't we?"

"Yes, we do," Sadie said. "Including the *Chronicle*. So we should be busy. I have a second person coming in to help tomorrow, so you won't be alone."

"Oh, that's right! You've got the rescheduled event at Matteo's winery. You're driving up in the morning?"

"That was my plan," Sadie said. "But if we get the mark-downs under control, I could drive up today and see how Tina's doing." Sadie paused, looking around the shop. She nodded her head, satisfied with the plan, and then headed for the front door. "I'll be right back. I need to run over to Matteo's for a minute."

"Coconut truffle for me, while you're at it," Amber shouted after her.

* * *

Matteo's shop wasn't open for business yet, but as soon as Sadie tapped on the glass pane, he ushered her in, then resumed counting change into the cash register to prepare for customer traffic.

Sadie browsed the display cases and let Matteo finish setting up the register. As soon as he was organized, she picked out a few items for herself and Amber, plus an assortment of Matteo's much-loved miniature peanut butter pumpkins for Flair to have on hand at the following day's sale. The least she could do when she left her shop girls to cope with a sale without her was to make sure there was an adequate sugar supply.

"Any word from Tina today?"

"As a matter of fact, yes," Matteo said. "The police let her go again. She's home."

"I'm glad to hear that," Sadie said. "She's been dragged in there twice, and there isn't any real evidence against her. You know she thinks Stefano is setting her up."

"She told me the same thing. But she's just distraught. There's no reason Stefano would do that. He wouldn't have had any reason to kill Flanagan. Stefano was all for selling. And how would he have known Flanagan would be there?"

"How would anyone have known?" Sadie pointed out. *Except Matteo, who told him to meet there…*

Matteo shook his head, realizing the implication. "I know what that looks like, but obviously someone knew. Besides me, that is."

"Could Stefano have been upset at Flanagan because the sale fell through?"

Matteo shot Sadie a look of disbelief. "No, if anything, he'd be upset with *me* about that. I'm the one who blocked it."

"How upset was he?"

"Not enough to try to kill me, if that's what you're thinking. He would have liked the money, but it's not like he needed it. He does fine with his store. And I don't think he was all that heartbroken when the sale fell through. He thought it was a good business move, but that's all."

Pausing at the end of the counter, Sadie picked up the trade show magazine she'd noticed on a previous visit. Thumbing to the page with the blue and gold logo, she asked Matteo about the company.

"I've seen this logo before," Sadie ventured. "What company is this?"

Matteo glanced at the magazine Sadie was holding. "Oh, those guys? That's Culinary Specialty Products, a supply outfit. They sponsor a lot of the shows. Have tote bags for people to collect brochures, that kind of thing. I was at one of their shows this past week. I went by after I closed the shop."

Matteo handed Sadie the chocolate stash, packed into a small box with an elastic ribbon looped over two diagonally opposed corners.

"Do they make anything besides tote bags?" Sadie asked. "Say, pins, for example?"

"Probably. All those companies give away promotional items at shows, you know, tote bags, mugs, coasters, pins, pens. I don't care for that stuff myself, but some people collect every little thing they can find. As long as the price is right, of course: free."

"You must have some sort of example you can show me," Sadie said.

"Actually, no. Unless a sample is edible, I ignore it. I don't need a bunch of useless knick-knacks kicking around here."

"No, I guess you don't." Sadie glanced around at the already crowded shop.

Sadie returned to Flair and found many of the sale items already priced and the front window display in progress.

"Amber, I think I'll go ahead and drive up to St. Vin today. Will you be all right getting the store ready for tomorrow?"

"Sure! You know I love to be busy. And Maggie is coming in at 3, so things won't be too hectic for me."

"Good. I'm lucky to have you. Matteo told me Tina is home, and I know the inn has vacancies. Her business hasn't exactly been booming since the news about the murder started flying around. I have a few hunches I'd like to follow. And I think it's possible the killer might return to the scene of the crime."

"Tomorrow? With all those people around?"

"No better place to hide, my dear," Sadie smiled.

CHAPTER TWENTY-ONE

Sadie pulled into the parking lot of The Vintage Vine in the late afternoon after fighting northbound traffic out of San Francisco. By the time she finished helping Amber get set for the sale the next day and left Flair, rush-hour traffic had begun.

Tina greeted her at the door with a hug, "Nice to see a friendly face around here, especially one without a badge."

"Yes, you've had quite a week, haven't you?" Sadie was pleased to see Tina in good spirits.

"Longest week in my life, seriously," Tina agreed, showing Sadie inside. "But it seems the police are focusing their search elsewhere now, thank goodness."

"Do they have another suspect?" Sadie wondered if she'd missed part of the puzzle.

Tina shrugged. "Maybe, who knows? I'm just glad to be home."

"I'm sure you are."

"How does the Merlot room sound again?"

"Perfect."

Sadie filled out a registration form and took the key from Tina. One trip from the car to the room and she was settled in, as was Coco, who was content in her travel palace. Sadie set out Coco's china food and water dishes and returned to the lobby.

"I have to go by the lawyer's office," Tina said. "Want to come along?"

Sadie jumped at the offer. Nick Perry might know what the detectives knew, or at least some of what they knew. She could learn something just by listening to him talk with Tina. He might even be willing to answer a few questions about Tina's arrest and release, as long as Tina didn't mind. And Sadie had a sense Tina was beginning to trust her as much as Matteo did.

Tina's Honda CR-V was neat and tidy, as meticulously kept as The Vintage Vine. It seemed oddly incongruous to Sadie that someone so organized would be a murder suspect.

A brief chill ran up Sadie's spine at the thought, far-fetched as she felt it was, that she could be riding in a car with a killer. But her instincts all along had led her to believe Tina's story, at least about being innocent. Whether or not Stefano had set her up, as Tina claimed, was another matter. She still believed Mr. Collins was involved in some way. That Tina herself would have someone purposely plant an item connected with the murder in her home was absurd. No, unless Sadie's usual keen perception skills were way off, Tina was in the clear.

Nick Perry's office was located not far from Vines and Tines. The building looked every bit like a structure for legal firms – expensive and formidable without appearing presumptuous. An engraved sign in the lobby indicated suite numbers for various tenants.

Tina led the way to Nick Perry's office on the second floor. They entered the suite, passing a woman in her mid-thirties who was on her way out.

"Do stop by and try out our new menu," the woman said as the lawyer walked her to the door.

"I look forward to it," Nick said. "Especially that *moussaka* you've been talking about. It sounds delicious."

"And our *baklava*," the woman added. "You can't miss that." She lowered her voice to a whisper. "I grind the walnuts; that's my secret." She put one finger in front of her lips, smiled and slipped out the door.

Nick turned to greet Tina, who started to introduce Sadie, then stopped when it became obvious they'd already met.

"We bumped into each other at the police station the other day," Nick explained to Tina. "Lovely to see you again, Ms. Kramer."

"Please, call me Sadie."

"Sadie it is, then," Nick replied. He motioned toward his office, inviting both women to step inside. "That was Mrs. Stavros of Stavros Taverna. Excellent Greek food. You must try it, if you haven't."

The law office was spacious and exquisitely decorated. It had all the necessary trappings for a new client to feel confident hiring Nick Perry for business deals. Award plaques for the accomplishments of the wineries and restaurants he represented filled the upper half of one wall. Below those, sleek bottles of premium wines graced a long marble counter. A set of crystal goblets etched with grapevines promised a few sips of the area's finest creations. On the opposite wall, framed photographs portrayed enthusiastic scenes of opening celebrations around the area. The entire office screamed success, right down to the imported rug below the luxurious leather armchairs facing Nick's desk.

"You have a fabulous office," Sadie said as she took a seat. "I take it you specialize in winery and restaurant deals?" She turned her head toward the photographs to back up her question.

"Yes, I handle a lot of business for local vineyards and restaurants," Nick replied, "but I also take cases for individuals, depending on the situation." He glanced at Tina. It wasn't necessary to elaborate.

While Tina handed over the folder she'd brought along and began to talk to the lawyer, Sadie stood and wandered over to a tall bookcase and browsed the titles. Not surprisingly, legal handbooks and law reviews filled most of the shelves. A small section was devoted to wine encyclopedias and cookbooks from some of the local establishments, presumably those Nick had worked with. Or, Sadie pondered, potential projects for the future. Pre-acquisition research, perhaps?

As she flipped through a cookbook and perused a mouth-watering recipe for chocolate soufflé, Sadie listened to the voices behind her.

"These records show you received the call from Luisa's phone number at 9:46 a.m. last Saturday," Nick said. "This is the call that led you to the winery that morning?"

"Yes, that's correct," Tina said. "Luisa was overwhelmed with last minute preparations and needed boxes of supplies stored in the fermentation building. Since I was planning to go to the festival soon, anyway, I said I'd come a little early and bring the boxes to her in the tasting room."

"Well, it's good we have this documented," Nick said. "It shows you only went to the fermentation building because Luisa asked you to. You probably wouldn't have even been there if she hadn't called."

"I definitely wouldn't have been there, not that early," Tina pointed out. "I had an inn full of people, including Sadie." Tina paused to look over at Sadie, who raised her eyes from the soufflé recipe and nodded.

"Sadie, do you remember the phone call? That could come in handy," Nick said.

"I didn't hear the conversation, but I did see Tina take a phone call as breakfast was winding down," Sadie said, replacing the cookbook on the bookshelf and moving back to the chair in front of Nick's desk. "The assistant innkeeper took over the remaining breakfast duties so Tina could leave."

"That's right," Tina said.

"If you don't mind me asking," Sadie began, looking at Tina, "didn't it seem odd to you that Luisa called you for help? From what you've told me this week, the two of you don't have the best of relationships."

Tina looked at Nick then at Sadie. "It did seem odd. But you both already know I think Stefano set that up to get me to the fermentation building. All he had to do was suggest to Luisa that I should be helping. Stefano could have done that because he wanted me to find the..." Tina paused, finishing with, "Flanagan."

Nick shook his head and tapped a pencil against a legal pad on his desk. "I'm still not convinced Stefano would have enough reason to set you up for something as serious as murder. You've said he was jealous of Matteo, but enough to kill Flanagan just to get back at you? That's not going to hold up in court."

"Why not," Sadie asked. "It wouldn't be the first time jealousy was a motive for murder."

"True," Nick said

"Besides," Sadie continued. "How can you be certain it was Flanagan he meant to kill? Maybe Flanagan was an innocent bystander, in the wrong place at the wrong time."

"You think Matteo was the intended victim?" Nick stopped tapping his pencil and waited for an answer.

"It would make sense," Sadie pointed out. "Stefano didn't have a problem with Flanagan, did he?"

"Not that I know of," Nick said. "Everyone thought Flanagan was pushy, but mostly the family appreciated his devotion to the project. Stefano wanted the sale to go through."

"What did you think about the sale?" Sadie directed this question at Nick, who seemed taken aback by it.

"It's not my place to be pro or con when it comes to these deals," Nick said. "My job is to represent the clients' wishes, to explain the terms of the offer, and to make sure any legal paperwork is in order."

"But in this case, the clients' wishes varied, right? Because you had more than one client with different opinions."

Nick set the pencil down and leaned forward, forearms on his desk. "True, but in the end there was just one client, the Tremiato Winery. The discussions about whether or not to sell were between the family members themselves. I witnessed some of the discussions but mostly kept quiet unless someone asked for information regarding the contracts and the law."

"Be glad *you* weren't there, Sadie," Tina interjected. "This family tends to argue a lot, anyway. But that winery deal sent people over the top. All the resentments and grievances from over the years emerged during those discussions."

"Really?" Sadie said, intrigued that there might be a new angle to follow. Perhaps the crime had nothing to do with the winery deal at all, but rather involved something from the past that emerged during the decision-making process.

"Yes, really." Tina looked over at Nick. "You remember, Nick."

"I'm afraid I do, though I try my best to forget." Nick shook his head. "It's normal for family members or business partners to disagree; I'm used to that. But I've never seen anyone return to a grade school quarrel as part of negotiations."

"A grade school quarrel?" Sadie raised her eyebrows. That sounded extreme, even for the Tremiato siblings.

"Yes," Tina said. "That was Angelo referring to a dispute he and Luisa had back in school. Which was ridiculous. But those two have always been rivals. They both think the other one is getting an unfair advantage in almost every situation from the work they do at the winery to the size of their portion of lasagna at dinner. In the tasting room now, Luisa is always trying to take over, and Angelo is constantly forced to stand his ground."

"I've noticed that myself," Sadie said. "I don't see why they can't both share the work. Surely there's enough to go around."

"Yes, you'd think so," Nick said vaguely, replacing papers in Tina's folder. "Anyway," he continued, "thank you for bringing these phone records in, Tina. I think this will help."

Sadie was not at all surprised to see Nick change the subject. Since they were dating, it had to be difficult for him to stay objective when Luisa's name came up.

"And Sadie," Nick continued, reaching for a business card from a desktop stand. "you seem to have a knack for digging up information. If you think of anything that might help, please give me a call." He flipped the card over, picked up a blue and gold ballpoint pen and wrote his cell phone number on the back.

"I'll be sure to let you know if anything comes to mind," Sadie replied.

CHAPTER TWENTY-TWO

Sadie wrapped her hands around a cup of peppermint tea and looked around the dining room of The Vintage Vine. Like many bed and breakfasts she'd visited over the years, the surroundings reminded her of days gone by. The crocheted lace runner that adorned the buffet could have been the same one on her own grandmother's long dining room table. A china cabinet housed an assortment of tea cups worthy of a tearoom.

"Tina, tell me about the cork the detectives found in the kitchen."

A second cup of tea settled on the table as the innkeeper sat down. To Sadie's delight, Tina brought a plate of chocolate-dipped cookies with her. Sadie took one immediately, savoring the combined taste of peppermint and chocolate as she bit into the baked goodie.

"It was just a cork, the kind you normally find in a wine bottle."

Sadie nodded. "It did have the name of the winery on it. You mentioned that on the phone the other night. Is that unusual?"

"Not at all. The Tremiatos stamp the name of the winery on all their corks just like many wineries do. I don't think that would have been an issue, except…"

"Except," Sadie took over. "…it wasn't in the cabinet the first time they searched, so it appeared to have been moved, maybe hidden somewhere else in the house the first time they investigated."

"Right," Tina replied. "They asked me if I had moved it. Of course I hadn't, since it was never there in the first place."

"The type of wine was a problem, too?"

"Yes. It was a common wine, a cabernet, but it was the same type of wine found at the scene."

"I can see that wouldn't look good." Sadie took another cookie. "But there were no fingerprints on the cork itself."

"Right. That's why they let me go."

A pained expression crossed Tina's face. Sadie understood this. Thinking back to the discovery of Flanagan's body had to be disturbing. Sadie felt queasy thinking about it and she hadn't even been inside the fermentation building.

"How do they know it was from the same bottle? The police wouldn't give me any details." This was something that always irritated Sadie. The authorities never wanted to divulge facts to her, yet expected her to provide them with information.

"There were traces of glass in the cork," Tina said.

"Couldn't that have been from any bottle?"

"Not really. Glass doesn't fragment into the wine or corks."

"Unless you hit someone over the head with a bottle." Sadie quickly revised her wording when she saw Tina's face. "I don't mean *you*. I mean if 'someone' hits someone else over the head."

"I knew what you meant," Tina said. "I'm just tired of being suspected of something I didn't do. I never should have agreed to go help Luisa that morning."

"You had no way of knowing you were walking into that situation," Sadie pointed out.

"That's what puzzles me," Tina said, reaching for a cookie herself. "Luisa never asks me to help with anything. She's determined to do everything on her own."

"I can see that. It's obvious she resents Angelo taking control of the tasting room."

"She resents everything," Tina laughed. "She's one of the unhappiest, angriest people I've ever known. Don't let her quiet demeanor fool you."

"Don't worry, it doesn't. But I find it odd she called you that morning."

"Well, it was a big event – *is* a big event. She might have just been overwhelmed with last minute details. She might have felt a little desperate. If she'd asked Angelo for help, he could have used her request against her to get even more control over the business. She also may not have wanted to bother Mama Elena, who might have assumed Luisa wasn't organized enough."

"Maybe." Sadie said, unconvinced. She was always suspicious when people's actions deviated from the norm. "Tina, if someone did set you up, could it have been Luisa?"

Tina opened her mouth to answer, but the phone rang. She picked up the receiver, paused, and then slammed it back into the cradle.

"Reporters! Can't they just leave me alone?" Tina sat back down, hands pressed against her forehead.

"Isn't this going to be a problem tomorrow?" Sadie asked. "You might be hit hard at the festival."

Tina shook her head. "I'm not going, even though Nick said he would have some people at the entrance who would try to screen out reporters."

"I'd think that would be hard to do," Sadie said. "It would be easy for a reporter to pass as any other attendee."

"Exactly. And I'm tired of being in the public eye." Tina picked up her empty tea cup, as well as Sadie's. "More tea?"

Sadie shook her head as she stood. "No, thanks. I'm going out to find dinner in a bit. I think I'll run by The Grapevine again. I'm rather addicted."

"Good idea. They always have a wonderful Friday night special." Tina smiled and disappeared into the kitchen, leaving Sadie to head back to the Merlot room.

* * *

Dressed in a bright lime tunic with a glittery peacock motif, Sadie clipped turquoise baubles on her ears. She'd always been fond of green, the brighter, the better. Slipping on metallic silver flats to pick up the sparkle above, she lifted Coco from her palace and settled the dog into her tote bag. She glanced at her figure in the mirror and smiled, satisfied that she looked like her normal, flamboyant self.

Sadie was surprised to find The Grapevine abuzz with activity. She found, in general, that popular lunch places were not necessarily popular dinner places, but this café had clearly managed to succeed at both meals so well that there was a waiting list to get in. Too hungry to sign in and hope for a table within the next hour, she headed to the counter, which didn't require a wait. Another diner was saving one of the two unoccupied seats for a friend, so Sadie took a spot two spaces down.

A server with a nametag that simply said "Glad" placed a dinner menu in front of her, along with a tiny plate of antipasti. She pointed to a chalkboard with the Friday night special, and rushed off to ring up an order to go.

"My, Coco," Sadie whispered into the tote bag on her lap, "This young girl has the entire counter to handle, plus the register." When she raised her head, she found a woman sitting in the seat closest to hers was staring at her.

"Does it talk back?"

Sadie studied the expression on the thirty-something woman's face. At times, talking to Coco when the pup was in her tote led to entertaining exchanges with strangers. But she could tell this wasn't going to be one of them. The contemptuous look on the woman's face didn't instill a desire for a friendly chat.

"Sometimes. Sometimes it even picks up the tab."

There, Sadie thought to herself. *That should do it.* A more endearing neighbor might have earned a more forthcoming answer, even an introduction to the canine princess hiding inside the bag. But this wasn't one of those times.

Sadie was relieved to see the woman turn away to greet her approaching friend. As the two women settled in at the counter and chattered hellos to each other, Sadie perused her menu. Although the range of dishes looked appealing, the dinner special on the chalkboard won out. The rich fettuccine alfredo with garlic bread was sure to be filling, and the carbs promised a decent night's sleep. If the following day went the way she hoped it would, she would need her rest. She placed her order and took a green olive for herself from the petite plate of appetizers, as well as a slender carrot stick, which she casually slipped into her tote bag.

"I think she's guilty."

The sudden comment from the woman next to her surprised Sadie. Looking up, she realized the woman wasn't speaking to her, but to her friend. Always eager for a chance to eavesdrop, Sadie took another olive and listened.

"I don't think so," the second woman replied. "There are other Tremiatos who seem like more obvious culprits to me."

"How do you figure?" the first woman asked. "Stefano's wife discovered the body – can you even imagine? – and I heard they found evidence in her bed and breakfast."

"That tiny little goody-two-shoes? She's not strong enough. Didn't the news reports say the victim was hit over the head? Maybe it was Stefano. He's got some muscles on him."

"I certainly hope it wasn't him. Locking up eye candy like that would be a crime!"

Both women giggled. Sadie rolled her eyes.

"Then again, it could have been Luisa. Everyone knows she and that lawyer have been fooling around together. Maybe the man who died saw him sneaking out of her place one night and confronted her. Luisa might have panicked, worrying that Elena would find out. You know, that old-fashioned mother of theirs? The one who never misses Mass?"

The second woman responded. "I can't see it. Luisa was always icy, even back in high school. But murder? That's too far-fetched."

Sadie, too, had considered that the Tremiato sister could have done the killing. Like all of the family members, she had the opportunity and she had a more powerful build than Tina. Luisa had sided with her mother against the sale, which would have made Flanagan's persistent pressure to sell aggravating, but by the time of the murder, the Tremiatos had already decided to keep the winery in the family. Once Matteo ended the negotiations, Flanagan didn't have any power. Luisa had no reason to see him as a threat. Sadie doubted Nick Perry was sneaking in or out of Luisa's back door even if they *were* an item. Also, Matteo hadn't told anyone he was meeting Flanagan in the fermentation building, so Luisa wouldn't have known to be there. Only Matteo and Flanagan knew about the meeting. Which brought Sadie right back to the one possibility she least liked. Was Matteo guilty after all? Or…could someone else have known about the meeting?

A small salad of arugula and red leaf lettuce, topped with thinly sliced cucumber and fresh cherry tomatoes, interrupted Sadie's thoughts. She drizzled feta vinaigrette dressing over it from a miniature pitcher with a deep blue glaze. Taking a bite, she closed her eyes and sighed with content. She loved food. There was no way around it. Fancy, plain, calorie-laden or healthy, she never tired of the infinite combination of flavors that could be found in an edible creation.

The women beside her pulled her out of her gustatory reverie when she heard the name "Tremiato" again.

"You know," said the one who had caught Sadie talking to her tote bag, "I wouldn't put it past any of those Tremiatos to kill someone. Except for Luisa, they're all a hot-blooded bunch."

Her friend laughed. "You think? Even Angelo?"

"Yes, even Angelo." She paused to sip her wine, and Sadie wondered if she were drinking the Tremiato chardonnay. "I dated him in high school for a couple of months."

"No! Really? I've always thought of him as a milder, geekier, oilier version of his older brothers."

Sadie pretended she was consumed with dabbing her bread into her sauce rather than memorizing every word.

"I know he comes across as being nearly as much of a cold fish as his sister, but Angelo has quite the temper, especially when he doesn't get what he wants. At least he did when he was seventeen."

And that was the end of it. The friends started gossiping about other people they dated in high school, other people they used to know, retold stories about cheerleading pranks and then moved on to a debate about some person on a reality television show.

Sadie wasn't interested in such silly subjects, and she stopped listening. As she pondered the possibility that the impassive Angelo might have the heart of a killer, she wound her way through the fettuccine, enjoying every last swirl of her fork. She passed up the server's dessert suggestion, knowing she was almost past her limit with the parmesan-crusted garlic bread that accompanied the pasta.

After she paid her bill, she left for The Vintage Vine. Impulsively, she decided to detour by Vines and Tines on the chance that Stefano might be working late, though she wasn't sure he had anything more to tell her about the events at the winery last weekend. If nothing else, she could do some window shopping at the cute pet store next door. She hadn't yet been able to stop in to see if she could add to Coco's rhinestone collar collection. She only had pink, purple, silver and gold to choose from. Or maybe she'd catch a glimpse of a new toy, an alternative to the much-loved red rubber hedgehog and the octopus that traveled with them...a stuffed frog, perhaps?

Sadie pulled over to the curb and parked. As she turned off her engine and prepared to climb out of the car, she noticed a faint light coming from inside Vines and Tines. The front lights were all off, and the store was obviously closed for the night, but when she looked through the front window she could see that the office door behind the sales counter was open. She could make out the silhouette of a figure inside. *Nothing strange about that*, she thought. *It's just Stefano working late.* Tina had said Stefano spent most evenings away from the inn. Maybe his staying away wasn't personal at all. Could the business not be doing as well as everyone thought? Had Stefano needed the money from the sale more than he'd let on?

When Sadie got out of the car, she closed the door gently then walked up to Vines and Tines and tapped lightly on the glass to see if she could get Stefano's attention. Maybe she'd be able to catch him in a more vulnerable mood, one that would help her get more information out of him than he would get out of her. She thought she heard voices or at least *a* voice, and she waited. But the light went off, and no one came to the front. Her tapping must have been too faint, and he must have left by a back exit into the alley behind the row of shops. Sadie felt on edge as she started up the car and went back to the inn, all thoughts of window shopping for pet attire forgotten.

CHAPTER TWENTY-THREE

As Sadie entered the inn through the back door, she heard voices coming from the front room. She settled Coco into her palace in the Merlot room and made her way down the hallway. She felt a charge of pleasure at the thought that Tina had a walk-in guest. The lack of customers since the murder had to be a financial drain. Perhaps that was why Stefano was working after hours?

Sadie followed the voices to the dining room, where she found Tina and Stefano seated, just finishing a meal. Seeing the almost empty plates in front of the two puzzled her until she realized it meant just what it appeared to mean: Stefano had been at the inn for some time. He couldn't possibly have been the figure inside Vines and Tines. *If not Stefano, then who?*

"Sadie, have some coffee with us," Tina said as Sadie entered. "We're just finishing up dinner." Tina stood to remove plates from the table. "And I have a key lime pie for dessert."

"I couldn't eat a single bite now," Sadie laughed. "That fettuccine alfredo and garlic bread at The Grapevine was enough to last me all week. Well, at least until tomorrow."

"Oh, yes, very filling. It's one of my favorite specials there," Stefano said. "But you'll want your appetite back for the Harvest Festival. Luisa always puts out a great spread for visitors."

"Yes, I remember," Sadie answered. "Maybe a cup of coffee would be nice."

She hated to disturb what seemed like a rare evening of camaraderie between the two of them. Maybe their marriage wasn't as much of a mess as she'd thought. But she felt obliged to let Stefano know she'd seen activity at his shop.

"Stefano, I was wondering, did you leave Vines and Tines to someone else to close up tonight?"

"Did you hire someone new?" Tina asked as she returned from the kitchen with three steaming coffee mugs on a tray.

"No. I always close up. I'm a little controlling when it comes to cashing out and making sure everything is locked. Why do you ask, Sadie?"

Sadie sat down and pulled one of the mugs to her though she didn't feel like drinking coffee. "I drove by your store on my way back to the inn just a few minutes ago, and could have sworn I saw a light on and someone moving around in your office."

Stefano and Tina exchanged a glance that Sadie couldn't quite interpret.

"That's not possible. I've been here for at least two hours, and I'd already locked up myself. Are you sure you saw someone?"

Sadie was starting to get a headache from all the seemingly unconnected bits of data swirling around in her brain. "Yes. I mean, no. I don't really know, but I thought I saw a light and a silhouette of a person in your store."

Tina put down her mug with a firm clink. "Maybe we should go check, Stefano. Or call the police."

Stefano waved away Tina's suggestion. "I would think you'd had enough of the police, my dear. I can go on my own."

"Why don't we all go," Sadie said.

They left the cooling mugs of coffee on the table and all piled into Tina's Honda, Sadie in the back where she watched the younger people for signs that they knew something they weren't saying aloud. She wished Coco were with her, though she would have hesitated to consult with her canine partner in front of the couple.

Tina parked on the street in front of Vines and Tines, and the three of them stood on the sidewalk for a moment, peering through the shop's clean window.

"I think the office door is open, Stefano, though I could just be seeing a shadow," Tina said.

"Well, I might have left that door ajar. I was eager to get home to you."

Sadie stifled a snort. She wasn't completely buying this sudden change in Stefano's attitude toward his wife. "Why don't we go inside to see if anything is missing or moved," she said.

Stefano jingled his keys on their ring until he found the one that unlocked his shop. He opened the door and stepped inside. "I know ladies should be first, but in this case...."

He flipped on the lights and called out. "Anyone here? It's Stefano." He crossed behind the counter and went into the office, Sadie and Tina close behind him.

Stacks of papers and trade journals spilled onto the floor near a desk cluttered with pens, scraps of note paper and a travel mug tilted on its side.

"It looks like someone has been rifling through the things on your desk, Stefano," Sadie said.

Tina clutched Sadie's arm and looked behind her as if a shadow might leap out at them from one of the corners. Polished tables and elegant china became monsters in the low light.

Stefano laughed. "No, no, my desk is just the way I left it. I don't think anything is out of place."

"How can you tell?" Sadie asked as she backed away from the mess.

"What's that on your chair?" Tina moved around both Sadie and Stefano and plucked a silver Cross pen from one of the leather folds. She waved it in the air at her husband. All Sadie could think was, *Tina! You're getting your fingerprints all over that glossy surface.* "Is this yours? Did one of your little groupies give it to you?"

Stefano slapped his right hand against his chest over his heart. "I'm wounded! You know you are my only one. I just like ... to ..."

Sadie finished for him. "Flirt?"

"Yes! And, no, that is not my pen, though I may have accidentally borrowed it from a customer signing a credit card slip. I get so busy I sometimes don't know what one hand is doing while the other waves. It might even be Angelo's. I think he has one like it. I might have pocketed it by accident."

Sadie dug into the pocket of her slacks and found a folded tissue. "Here. Why don't we wrap this up just in case someone broke in and left it here? The police might be able to dust it for prints or something." Sadie folded the pen into the tissue like it was a wine goblet and tucked it away. She looked around the small office and noticed that despite the mass of paper and array of junk, there was a kind of an organization to it. The filing cabinets each had a label marked with letters on a crisp white card. One of the drawers was open slightly, and Sadie could see the edge of a blue file folder.

"Do you tend to forget to shut your file drawers, too, Stefano?" she asked.

He frowned and looked where she pointed. "No. That I do not do. My financials are in those cabinets, and other confidential information related to the business."

"Maybe we should call the police, after all," Sadie said.

"No!" Stefano and Tina said the word simultaneously. "It's fine," Stefano said. "I probably was just being careless. I think everything is fine here. We should go back to the inn to get some rest so that we can all enjoy tomorrow's festival."

Sadie had no choice but to follow Stefano and Tina out of the store and back into Tina's car. While they drove the short distance back to The Vintage Vine, Sadie pondered their behavior. Maybe they were just tired of police intrusion in their lives, as Stefano had suggested. Maybe they were afraid Stefano's files would reveal something embarrassing or incriminating. Maybe Stefano had never tried to set up Tina. Or maybe Stefano and Tina were in on some kind of plot together.

Back at the inn, Tina gathered the mugs full of cold coffee and returned them to the kitchen. "Would you like me to brew a fresh pot of coffee?" she called.

"Sure," Stefano said.

Sadie didn't answer. She sat at the table resting her chin in her hands feeling suddenly exhausted.

"I am looking forward to the Harvest Festival," she said, wondering if the chocolate-covered cream puffs had been ordered again. Not that she cared all that much at the moment, love of chocolate aside. She was far more interested in seeing if the killer would return to the scene of the crime. "I think I'll pass on more coffee." She pushed her chair back and stood. "I think that visit to your store wore me out, Stefano. A solid night's rest sounds good right about now."

"I understand," Tina said. "By the way, Stefano has convinced me to go to the festival tomorrow." She poured coffee into mugs for Stefano, as well as herself, and set the third mug aside.

"Yes," Stefano said. "Tina shouldn't have to miss it just because of rumors and media coverage. I trust Nick to cover all the bases."

Sadie watched Stefano as he spoke. He sounded sincere. She was ever more certain that he had not framed Tina or set her up to take the blame for Flanagan's death. Whether he was guilty of murder or not was another question, but nothing in Stefano's behavior now indicated he felt Tina should be considered at fault. He cared about her too much to make her take the fall for something he'd done. If he'd actually done anything.

"You'll be there tomorrow, right, Sadie?" Stefano took a sip of coffee, eyeing Sadie over the rim of his mug. He laid his free hand gently on Tina's arm.

Sadie looked back and forth between the two, wondering what had instigated this shift in their treatment of each other but glad for it. She faked a yawn.

"Don't worry. I wouldn't miss it for all the chocolate in Belgium."

Back in her room, she traded her day clothes for leopard print pajamas and made just one phone call, reaching voice mail. She left a quick message before slipping into bed.

"Detectives, I think you're going to want to be at the Harvest Festival tomorrow."

CHAPTER TWENTY-FOUR

Fresh squeezed orange juice and a plate of baked goods greeted Sadie when she arrived in the breakfast area the following morning, but there was no sign of Tina. Instead, next to the coffee urn, Sadie found a note saying the innkeeper would see her at the festival. Sadie was to help herself to anything else she needed from the kitchen. It struck Sadie as ironic that Tina would choose to venture out before the event was scheduled to begin, seeing how it had backfired so dramatically the week before. Personally, Sadie would have hesitated to repeat the unlucky pattern.

After juice, coffee and two raspberry scones, Sadie took Coco out for a short walk and then returned to the Merlot room to prepare for the day. Reassuring Coco that she'd be taking her to the festival, Sadie set out clothes for the event. She'd packed for the season, bringing silky brown slacks and a matching gold belt and shoes. Three clattering strands of glass beads in sunset hues added variety to a bright coral blouse, as did additional beads dangling from her earlobes. She finished the outfit off by wrapping a multi-colored silk scarf around her head, knotting it over one ear and letting its leafy print trail down over her shoulder.

"Here you go, Coco." Sadie set the Yorkie in her lap and traded her pink rhinestone collar for one in gold. "Now we match each other, except you are far cuter." She kissed Coco's head and got her situated in the tote bag, making sure the velvet pillow inside was adequately fluffed. Receiving an enthusiastic wag of approval, Sadie gathered her things, including the tissue-wrapped pen, and left for the festival.

* * *

An active scene greeted Sadie at the Tremiato Winery. Between the usual draw of the event and the recent media coverage, it was clear most everyone in search of good food, good wine, or good gossip was going to be there. Arriving only ten minutes after the festival's opening time, Sadie found the parking lot outside the tasting room already full. Additional parking for the day in a dirt area allowed her to grab a space. If she'd arrived fifteen minutes later, she would have been faced with parking alongside the long driveway and walking back up to the main grounds. It appeared people would be parking out on the highway soon.

Sadie made her way across the grounds toward the tasting room, taking her time to look around. There was no sign of Tina or any of the other Tremiato siblings. Most of the mingling crowd appeared to be tourists, identifiable by their cameras and area maps. Their likely plan was to enjoy the festival and then hit a few other wineries later in the day. A few locals littered the grounds, as well. By now Sadie recognized several faces from the meals she'd eaten at The Grapevine. She was certain she spotted the two chatty ladies who'd sat next to her at the counter the night before. And Detectives Hudson and Shafer were there, out of uniform, blending in seamlessly with those around them.

The tasting room was already full. Sadie was happy to see the family had ordered the same appetizer spread from the week before. She grabbed a stuffed mushroom and looked around, finally spotting a Tremiato as he approached her.

"Here you go." Stefano donned one of his classic smiles as he handed Sadie a glass of what she guessed would be chardonnay. One sip told her she was right.

"Thank you, Stefano," Sadie said. "Looks like you're going to have quite a crowd today."

"Yes, I think you're right," Stefano replied, turning his head slightly as two attractive women eyed him on the way to the appetizer table. Sadie had to admit he looked dapper in his crisp khaki trousers and light blue button-down shirt, sleeves rolled up.

"Where is Tina?"

"What do you mean, where is Tina?" Stefano looked puzzled.

"She left me a note saying she'd see me here. I assumed she'd come here to help with preparations."

"She had to stop by Nick Perry's office," Stefano said. "But she's here now. I saw her car pull in a few minutes ago.

"Yes," Luisa said, joining Sadie and Stefano. "Nick called here this morning, looking for her." She paused, holding out a ceramic platter. "Bruschetta?"

Sadie readily accepted the appetizer. She'd polished off the stuffed mushroom even before her first sip of chardonnay. She'd have to pace herself if she wanted to save room for cream puffs later.

"I'm surprised she even planned to come today," Luisa added. "Considering what she's been through, that is. I'd be inclined to hide out."

"Luisa, she has no reason to hide. She hasn't done anything wrong," Stefano said. "But at least you didn't ask her to help out here like you did last week. That didn't go too well."

"No, it certainly didn't," Luisa said. "I should have just done everything myself, like I always do."

"Stefano," Sadie interrupted, glad for an excuse to ask something she'd been wondering. "Aren't you the one who suggested Luisa call Tina for help last week?"

Both Luisa and Stefano looked at Sadie, confused,

"No," Stefano said. "Why would you think that? I didn't know Luisa needed help. She usually manages to do the work of five women instead of one."

Luisa smiled at her younger brother.

Sadie bit her lip, searching for a quick answer. Saying that Tina thought he'd suggested the call to set her up was out of the question. Fortunately, Luisa spoke before Sadie was forced to stumble into an awkward answer.

"My calling Tina was Nick's idea," Luisa said. "I was running short on time that morning and he saw me panicking. He said I was taking too much on myself and I should ask Tina to help, to let her do her share of the work. This time we hired extra staff." She paused, looking around. "Speaking of Nick, he must be here somewhere."

Luisa moved away, mingling with the growing crowd, welcoming visitors and passing out bruschetta. Angelo had taken a place at the counter by now and was pouring generous portions of wine into glasses with the Tremiato name etched on the side. A sign announced free souvenir glasses, one each with the purchase of a bottle of wine. The enthusiastic group gathered around Angelo proved the promotion was a smart marketing tactic. Several guests had already claimed four wine bottles in order to score a set of four glasses.

Elena appeared, dressed in a modest skirt and blouse, with a shawl around her shoulders. Her serenity was a stark contrast to last week's flustered anger. Stefano took his mother's arm and led her to a chair, which a guest readily vacated when she saw the elderly woman approaching. Aside from her age, there was something about the Tremiato matriarch that commanded respect.

Sadie slipped into the tasting room, hoping for a minute of Angelo's time. He looked as happy as she'd ever seen him in their short acquaintance, competently filling glasses, popping corks, wiping spills off the smooth surface with a bar rag. As if he could feel her watching him, he looked up and smiled at Sadie, then handed a bottle to a short, blonde server and moved to the end of the counter to meet her.

"I'm so glad you were able to make it back to our vineyards, Sadie. What a change from last week, huh?"

"Indeed," Sadie said and reached into her silky slacks for the silver Cross pen. "I think you might have dropped this in Stefano's shop." She watched his face closely. "It is yours, isn't it?" Sadie held the pen toward him but didn't let it go.

She was surprised when Angelo let out a hearty laugh. "Yes! This is my pen, but I didn't drop it at Vines and Tines. Stefano is always 'accidentally' forgetting to return this pen to me when we get together to sign for deliveries or business papers. It's a running joke between us. It was part of an award I won in high school for community service. Stefano always thought *he* should have won that award."

"So you weren't in Stefano's shop last night after it was closed?"

Angelo shook his head. "No. I was here making sure Luisa didn't give our temporary workers nervous breakdowns and preparing the tasting room for the festival. I didn't have time to leave the property."

Sadie handed the pen to Angelo who bowed his head and slipped it into his shirt pocket.

"I'll let you get back to work, then," Sadie said.

"You call this work? I call this life," he said, and it occurred to Sadie that despite the jockeying for power between Angelo and Luisa, despite the sniping and complaining, both of them really did love the winery and the work they did there.

A brief jostling in her tote bag alerted Sadie to the fact a band had started up outside on the patio. Recognizing the song as "Volare," another of Coco's least favorites, she moved to the back door of the tasting room and stepped outside, farther away from the music. "I promise to set up a salsa-mambo medley on your iPod later," she whispered into the bag as the little dog settled down.

"You know, the winery is actually pet friendly. You don't need to keep it hidden."

Sadie turned to see Nick Perry leaning against the side of the building.

"Coco is a '*she*,' and prefers to be referred to by her own name."

"Well, in that case, let Coco out so she can enjoy the full experience." Nick grinned, and Sadie wondered if he was being serious or not.

"It's not that simple," Sadie explained. "She despises Dean Martin."

Nick laughed then, showing his white teeth and a set of dimples Sadie suspected might have been part of why Luisa had fallen for him. "I find that hard to believe," Nick ventured. "No one hates Dean Martin."

"Yes, many people do."

"But *Coco* is not a person."

Sadie could never quite understand why people were puzzled that Coco had such definite opinions about music, "Nice crowd," she said, eager to change the subject before she popped Nick in the nose. "And no one seems put off by the events of last week. It's almost as if it never happened."

"I was thinking the same thing," Nick said. "Maybe it will just fade away. That would be nice for the Tremiatos."

"You don't think Tina will end up being indicted?"

"I doubt it at this point," Nick said. "But even if she is, it should be easy to get the charges dropped. All the evidence is circumstantial."

"You really support this family, don't you?"

Nick looked surprised at Sadie's statement. "Well, yes, of course I do. First of all, that's my job as their lawyer. And, second of all, they're a good family."

"Especially certain ones?" Sadie smiled at the young attorney.

"Yes, Ms. Kramer," Nick said. "I'm not completely unbiased, as I'm sure you know by now. But Luisa and I are very good at keeping business and personal matters separate."

"I don't doubt it," Sadie said. "Speaking of which…"

"There you are," Luisa said, stepping out of the tasting room's back door. "I was looking for you earlier."

"I had to stop by the office on my way here." Nick kissed Luisa's cheek, and the Tremiato sister betrayed her ice queen reputation by blushing a bit. "Sorry to be late."

"I was just worried," Luisa added. "I haven't heard from you for a couple of days. I even called your sister, so you'll have to apologize for me the next time you see her."

"You called my sister?"

"I'm sorry," Luisa said. "Now I feel silly about it. I shouldn't have bothered her. Besides, I think she was confused. She said she hadn't seen you since you stopped by before some costume party earlier this week. What costume party?"

Nick laughed. "She was definitely confused. A bunch of guys from the law building were getting together for a happy hour Halloween shindig, but I didn't go. I must have mentioned it in passing." Although Nick was still smiling, Sadie thought the smile hadn't reached his eyes. He looked into the tasting room, waved at someone, and excused himself.

Sadie turned back to Luisa. "Lawyers, hmm? Can't live with 'em, can't live without 'em."

The expression that crossed the Tremiato sister's face was the warmest smile Sadie had yet seen on her. Sadie knew the look of someone smitten.

"Lawyers, indeed," Luisa said. "If it's not golf it's happy hour, or breakfast meetings, or art openings, or a dozen other social events. It's hard to believe they ever have time to file briefs or make objections or whatever work they do all day." She sighed and excused herself. "I need to check on our mother."

Sadie wandered back through the tasting room and out to the front courtyard. As expected, the crowd was growing quickly, with cars now parking along the lower half of the long driveway. The band had just finished one instrumental and was starting into another. Tina had joined Stefano and was sipping wine and swaying to the music.

A well-dressed server passed by with a tray of miniature quiches. Sadie took one delicately from the platter and then slyly swiped a second. Just before he walked away, she abruptly grabbed the entire tray, thanked the server and proceeded across the courtyard.

Pausing to offer appetizers to a few guests on the way, she approached Detectives Shafer and Hudson and insisted they each take a quiche, whispering across the tray as they did. Continuing through the crowd, she circled around to Nick, who also accepted the offering. Sadie waited patiently while he took a bite.

"So what do you think of the quiche, Nick?"

"Delicious," he said with his full mouth. "The Tremiatos know how to put on a good spread."

"They do, don't they, Nicolo? I've always admired the Italian love of food."

Sadie noticed that Nick's right eye twitched. "That's your name, right? Nicolo Perino-Serrano.

Nick took a step back, a motion that looked awkward compared to the lawyer's usual graceful and confident movements. "I don't know what you're talking about."

"Oh, I think you do," Sadie said.

Detectives Shafer and Hudson stepped forward, one from each side, where they'd been positioned behind Nick.

"It took me some time to figure this out, but you resented Flanagan," Sadie continued. "You wanted that sale to go through and he couldn't make it happen."

"Flanagan was an idiot!" Nick snarled. "But I didn't go there to meet him."

"Then who did you go to meet?"

"I went to see Matteo, to intercept the evidence he was going to pass on to him. I thought I could talk him down, keep him from telling Flanagan the truth about my grandfather."

"About the embezzling," Sadie filled in. "And you came to the winery that night because you bugged Simon Flanagan's phone and heard their plan to meet."

"Yes. But Matteo wasn't even there."

"But Flanagan was," Sadie said. "And you confronted him."

"I had to! He was flaunting the fact he'd finally be able to prove his father's innocence. I couldn't let that happen!"

A crowd began to gather, many of the guests whispering to each other.

"I don't think that's all of it," Sadie said. "He also threatened to make it public that you were really a part of Serrano-Flanagan, didn't he? He was going to tell everyone you were working both sides of the acquisition deals, which was a conflict of interest and would have affected your position as an attorney."

"Yes!" Nick yelled. "Don't you see? That would have ruined me. He wouldn't stop pushing. So smug, that little weasel of a salesman. After all I'd done for him over the years. Just like the Serranos have *always* done for the Flanagans – giving them more of the business than they deserve. Then he thinks he can stab me in the back? Take everything I've worked for away?"

"No, I suppose that wouldn't have been good at all," Sadie said. She tapped a finger against her pursed lips. Sunlight reflected off a flashy cluster of topaz on her ring finger. "So in your anger, you grabbed the nearest item, a bottle of wine. You hit him over the head and the bottle broke, cutting his neck. You tried to move him, realized he was dead, and panicked and ran. But then you went back to retrieve the bottleneck, knowing your prints would be on it. That's when you wiped the doorknob clean.

"Later you disguised yourself as Mr. Collins by having your sister do your makeup for a non-existent costume happy hour. You went to The Vintage Vine, checked in, and hid the cork in the kitchen cabinet and then left in the middle of the night, to make Tina look guilty."

"That wasn't me! I don't know any Mr. Collins!"

Sadie ignored him and continued. "I heard you and saw you leave that night. You knew Stefano would go by to see how Tina was doing. It could easily look like he planted the cork, since you knew he was jealous of Matteo. So you set Stefano up to look like *he* was setting Tina up, all to cover your tracks."

Luisa, who had been standing nearby, stunned, spoke for the first time. "Nick, is this true? Tell me she's wrong!"

Nick stared directly into Luisa's eyes for a moment then looked away.

"I'm afraid she's right. He played both of us," Stefano said, stepping to his sister's side and directing a furious look at the family lawyer. "There *was* someone in my shop last night, wasn't there, Nick, or Nicolo?" Stefano's voice was taunting as he used the lawyer's Italian name. "What were you doing there? Were you planting more false clues?"

"No! I was looking for the information Matteo planned to give to Flanagan! You Tremiatos might pretend to hate each other, but I know you're a tight family. You must have been working with Matteo to hide that proof from me!"

Stefano blinked once. "I have no idea what you're talking about. I haven't even spoken to Matteo recently. But I do know one thing now. You are a horrible, despicable man. Offering me your false friendship is one thing, Nick, Nicolo, or whoever you are. But taking advantage of my sister is another. And because of you, my wife had to spend time in a jail cell!" He pulled his right arm back and attempted a swing at Nick's jaw, but Detective Hudson blocked the blow.

"We'll take care of this," Hudson said, holding Stefano back.

"Nicolo Perino-Serrano, you're under arrest for the murder of Simon Flanagan," Detective Shafer said, slapping handcuffs around Nick's wrists and continuing to read him his rights.

Stefano shook free of Detective Hudson and backed off, turning to Sadie. "How did you know?"

Sadie stepped forward, knowing the lawyer's wrists were now firmly cuffed. She reached into Nick's shirt pocket and pulled out a ballpoint pen, holding it up for others to see.

"A pen?"

"Not just any pen," Sadie said, twisting it sideways so the logo on it showed. "This pen is from Culinary Specialty Products, a company that specializes in restaurant marketing." She turned back to Nick. "You used this pen yesterday to write on the back of the business card you gave me."

"So what?"

"So, it matches this," Detective Shafer said, pulling a small evidence bag out of her pocket. She held the bag up, showing the small pin that was found at the crime scene. It matched the logo on the pen.

"Oh!" Tina gasped. "That pin."

"You didn't say you recognized it when we showed it to you," Detective Hudson said. His voice was half understanding and half reprimanding.

"I didn't think it could have been Matteo's," Tina said. "I had no idea he'd been up here."

"I knew the pin wasn't Matteo's," Sadie added, "though I recognized that company's catalog at his shop. He's only one of thousands of people who attend those trade shows. And he doesn't collect the free merchandise handouts. Neither does Angelo, who also attended that show. But some people do." Sadie directed the last statement at Nick, who returned her gaze with a glare.

"How did you figure all this out, anyway?" Nick said.

"Well, you can thank Sal for that," Sadie said.

"Sal who?"

"No one you know," Sadie said. "Just a guy with good connections back in Boston who knew the original company name was Perino-Serrano Flanagan. I thought 'PSF' meant there were three partners, but it was just your family's hyphenated name that made it look that way. Eventually, the 'Perino' portion of the name was dropped. Conveniently, I imagine, when your father, Giancarlo Perino-Serrano, anglicized his name to John Serrano for the new company, doing the same with your name. You became Nick Perry."

"Time to go." Detective Hudson moved the crowd aside, forming a small aisle across the courtyard to a waiting squad car. Within minutes, the car was on its way to the police station.

Sadie took a glass of wine from a passing tray and held it up as she flipped her scarf behind her shoulder and faced the crowd.

"Wine, anyone?"

CHAPTER TWENTY-FIVE

"Did you see the new sign on Matteo's door? He posted new shop hours. He'll be closed every Sunday now." Amber handed Sadie a cup of coffee.

"Is that so?" Sadie raised her eyebrows at the news. "I'll have to go see what that's all about." She took a sip of the fresh brewed coffee and set it down on her desk, picking up the most recent sales reports. She scanned the column of items sold, pausing at one point to grin and hold out her hand, palm up.

"I knew you'd spot that right away." Amber laughed as she slapped a crisp ten dollar bill into Sadie's hand. "Mrs. Abernathy was thrilled with that extra discount on the purple sweater. She snapped it right up."

"I knew she would," Sadie said. "That woman was only waiting for one more sliver of savings."

After getting Coco settled in on the front counter's cushion, she went next door, where she found Matteo setting out a fresh tray of vanilla nut fudge for the day's customers.

"What's this about you being closed on Sundays from now on? I'm in chocolate withdrawal just thinking about it. Is this true"

Matteo nodded. "I've decided to spend Sundays at the winery now. Angelo and Luisa could use some help in the tasting room, since weekends are busy."

"I'll have to stock up on Saturdays to make sure I won't run out before Mondays, I suppose," Sadie said.

"I'll be glad to drop a small batch off to hold you over. I'll be packing up an assortment for the winery each week, as well."

"Now, that's good news," Sadie said, nodding with approval. "It's about time they started carrying your chocolates at the winery."

"Not just at the winery," Matteo said proudly. "Stefano is going to bring some into Vines and Tines, and Tina will be setting out a single truffle for each guest at night."

"I take it Stefano is fine with that," Sadie said.

Matteo smiled. "We talked our personal issues out on the phone after the police hauled that scumbag lawyer away."

"Wasn't that something," Sadie mused. "You never suspected Nick Perry was involved?"

"Not at all," Matteo admitted. "Our business dealings were either over the phone or through email. I hadn't talked to him since the negotiations for the sale ended. He'd always behaved admirably, so I had no reason to suspect him."

"To think Nick's law practice was a set-up from the start, a move on the part of Serrano-Flanagan to trick wineries into selling to them," Sadie said. "And that John Serrano, actually Giancarlo Peroni-Serrano, the one pressuring Flanagan all along, was Nick's father. You might have been able to figure that out sooner if Flanagan had been willing to reveal the name of the person threatening him. He might still be alive."

"I understand why he wouldn't tell me. That's not the kind of family you want to mess around with."

"Clearly." Sadie eyed a particularly appealing tray of caramel cashew clusters. "Poor Luisa. That was quite a shock for her."

"Don't worry, Luisa will land on her feet," Matteo laughed. "She's a tough one."

"Yes, I got that impression," Sadie smiled. "By the way, I talked to Tina last night, after I drove back here. She said the family's very grateful that you blocked the sale. In retrospect, that is. They credit you with keeping them from a huge mistake."

"The family business means a lot, to all of us Tremiatos. It's our tradition." Matteo's expression was strong and proud. "And now it will continue to be." He set out a row of small gold-foil boxes on the inside work counter and began to fill each with assorted truffles. "What about you, Sadie? What's next, now that you've solved the Flanagan murder?"

Sadie leaned forward and admired a tray of raspberry bark. She'd been known to enjoy a white chocolate creation now and then. Matteo's version was the best she'd ever tasted. She'd have to come back later in the day and pick some up.

"I have no idea, but I'm sure something will come up."

"Yes, Sadie." Matteo laughed. "You seem to have a knack for falling into these situations."

"Yes, Matteo, I suppose I do. But I wouldn't call it a knack. I believe I'd call it a flair."

"A flair, you say?" Matteo repeated. "As in a flair for your shop? A flair for chocolate?"

Sadie grinned as she headed to the door, stopping just briefly to look back at her favorite chocolatier and friend.

"Why, a flair for anything that comes along, my dear Matteo. Life is an adventure. I never know what's around the next corner, but I know there's something there."

"Yes, Sadie, knowing you, I'm sure there is."

Pate a Choux Recipe
For Cream Puffs

(Courtesy of Chef John Clover)

INGREDIENTS

- 1 ½ cups water

- 1 stick plus 1 tablespoon unsalted butter, cut into cubes

- 1 teaspoon sugar

- ½ teaspoon of salt

- 200 grams all-purpose flour (about 1 ½ cups)

- 8 large eggs

DIRECTIONS

1. Preheat the oven to 400°. Line 2 large baking sheets with parchment paper.

2. In a large saucepan, combine the water, butter, sugar and salt and bring to a boil. Reduce the heat to moderate. Add the flour all at once and stir vigorously with a wooden spoon until a tight dough forms and pulls away from the side of the pan, 2 minutes.

3. Remove the pan from the heat. In a bowl, beat 7 eggs and add to the dough in four batches, stirring vigorously between additions until the eggs are

completely incorporated and the pastry is smooth. The dough should be glossy and very slowly hang, stretch and fall from the spoon in thick ribbons. If necessary, beat in the remaining egg.

4. Transfer the dough to a piping bag fitted with a 1/2-inch plain tip. Pipe 1 1/2-inch mounds onto the baking sheets, leaving 1 inch between them.

5. Spray the mounds with nonstick cooking spray. Bake the *choux* for about 35 minutes, until browned and puffed, shifting the sheets from top to bottom and front to back halfway through. Let cool completely.

6. Using a serrated knife, slice off the tops and reserve. Fill the bottom halves with sweetened whipped cream and fresh raspberries, or Pastry Cream. Replace the tops, dust with confectioners' sugar and serve.

Pastry Cream Recipe

(Courtesy of Chef John Clover)

INGREDIENTS

- 2 cups whole milk

- 1/2 cup sugar

- 1/2 vanilla bean, split lengthwise, seeds scraped

- Pinch of salt

- 4 large egg yolks

- 1/4 cup cornstarch

- 2 tablespoons unsalted butter, cut into small pieces

DIRECTIONS

1. In a medium saucepan, combine milk, 1/4 cup sugar, vanilla bean and seeds, and salt. Cook over medium heat until mixture comes to a simmer.

2. In a medium bowl, whisk together egg yolks, cornstarch, and remaining 1/4 cup sugar. Whisking constantly, slowly pour about 1/2 cup of the hot-milk mixture into the egg-yolk mixture, 1/2 cup at a time, until it has been incorporated.

3. Pour mixture back into saucepan, and cook over medium-high heat, whisking constantly, until it thickens and registers 160 degrees on an instant-read thermometer, about 2 minutes. Remove and discard vanilla bean.

4. Transfer to the bowl of an electric mixer fitted with the paddle attachment. Add the butter, and beat on medium speed until the butter melts and the mixture cools, about 5 minutes.

5. Cover with plastic wrap, pressing it directly onto the surface of the pastry cream to prevent a skin from forming. Refrigerate until chilled, at least 2 hours or up to 2 days. Just before using, beat on low speed until smooth (you can also whisk by hand).

Chocolate Ganache

(Submitted by Samantha Anderson)

INGREDIENTS

- 6 oz. semi-sweet chocolate chips
- 1/2 cup heavy cream

DIRECTIONS

6. In a glass bowl, microwave chocolate about 2 minutes, taking out and stirring every 30 seconds, until just melted.

7. Add in heavy cream and microwave another 20 seconds.

8. Stir until smooth and drizzle over cream puffs.

ACKNOWLEDGEMENTS

Books only come to be through a network of people working together. *A Flair for Chardonnay* is no exception. I owe tremendous thanks to many family, friends and professionals for helping bring this story to life.

Elizabeth Christy deserves a vineyard of gratitude not only for her always exceptional editing, but for her brilliant help in developing Sadie Kramer's personality. Her patience with my often neurotic writing process is also commendable. Keri Knutson of Alchemy Book Covers has created a fun, colorful cover concept for the Sadie Kramer Flair Mysteries, beginning with this book, the first in the series. Leah Banicki is responsible for eBook and full-cover formatting. Credit goes to Tim Renfrow at Book Design and More for print formatting. Jay Garner, Karen Putnam and Carol Anderson provided insightful beta reading. Carol gets extra credit for her keen proofreading eye.

I owe special thanks to Susan Foppiano-Valera for giving me an inside view of the winery business, including a fascinating and educational tour of Foppiano Vineyards in Healdsburg, CA. In addition, Chef John Clover also kindly contributed by sharing recipes for pate a choux and pastry cream. Samantha Anderson graciously added the recipe for chocolate ganache.

Above all, I am grateful for my family, friends and readers, who provide constant support as I translate the crazy scenes in my head into stories. Sadie tells me you all deserve chocolate-drizzled cream puffs. I whole-heartedly agree.